RIO SONORA

RIO SONORA

A STORY OF THE ARIZONA RANGERS

J. REEDER ARCHULETA

IZZARD INK
PUBLISHING

IZZARD INK PUBLISHING
PO Box 522251
Salt Lake City, Utah 84152
www.izzardink.com

Names: Archuleta, J. Reeder, author.
Title: Rio Sonora : a story of the Arizona Rangers / by J. Reeder Archuleta.
Description: First edition. | Salt Lake City, Utah : Izzard Ink Publishing, [2022]
Identifiers: LCCN 2022024414 (print) | LCCN 2022024415 (ebook) |
ISBN 9781642280838 (hardback) | ISBN 9781642280821 (paperback) |
ISBN 9781642280845 (ebook)
Subjects: LCGFT: Western fiction.
Classification: LCC PS3601.R389 R56 2022 (print) |
LCC PS3601.R389 (ebook) | DDC 813/.6--dc23/eng/20220524
LC record available at https://lccn.loc.gov/2022024414
LC ebook record available at https://lccn.loc.gov/2022024415

Designed by Meighan Cavanaugh
Cover Design by Andrea Ho

First Edition

Contact the author at info@izzardink.com

Hardback ISBN: 978-1-64228-083-8
Paperback ISBN: 978-1-64228-082-1
eBook ISBN: 978-1-64228-084-5

This one is for Joelle, Michael,
and the lovely Miss Amador.

PROLOGUE

———◆———

The sharp noises of the night patrols echoed through the city streets and often woke the boys in the foundling home. The measured cadence of brogans on the cobblestones and the harsh Yankee voices drifted on the Mississippi fog through the brick walls of the home. It had been like this ever since the blue-clad army had come up the river in their gunboats and taken the city without a fight.

But on this night, a young boy named Owen woke to another sound in the home. Muffled sobbing and harsh whispers came from the other end of the room. He had learned to come awake slowly when there were night noises in the room, even though most of the time it was just the smaller boys lost in their nightmares. But sometimes it was the older bully boys doing bad things to the little ones in the dark. He lay still and listened, opening his eyes to small slits. Then he slowly turned over to look past the iron stove in the center of the room, and he could make out bulky shadows leaning over a bunk near the door that led to the dining hall. An older boy cursed quietly; above this oath, Owen heard a thin, high-pitched noise come from Ansel's bunk. Slowly, the keening softened to a sound like a small kitten mewing for food. Ansel and he were not close friends, but they were the same age, and Owen stared at the far end of the room, thinking of what he could do to stop the bully boys. Some of the older boys were still in their beds, where they raised up, looked over at the commotion, and then lay back, pulling the covers over their heads.

Owen slipped out of his bunk and walked quickly over the cold stone floor to Ansel's bunk.

"Hey!" he yelled as loud as he could. His challenge echoed off the brick walls in a young boy's squeak.

A tall, raw-boned blonde named Jack turned and looked at him. "Go back to bed!"

"Leave Ansel alone!" Owen held his fists up in front of himself.

Jack looked down at him and laughed. Then quick as a snake, he backhanded the small boy and sent him sprawling into the foot of a bunk on the other side of the center aisle. Owen was stunned, but he felt no pain. He got to his feet, jumped up on Jack's back, and began pulling his hair and biting his ears. Jack shook him off, and Owen slid across the floor, scraping skin off his right cheek. As he slowly pulled himself up, Owen saw that Jack had moved across the aisle to finish him. He rushed at Jack, his arms pumping furiously, but the taller boy reached down, picked him up, and held him in a bear hug. Owen could feel Jack's grip begin to cut off his breathing. Owen put his hands together, locking his fingers the way the brothers made the boys hold their hands at prayer, and brought this small double fist down on the bridge of Jack's nose. He heard Jack grunt, so he hit him again and panicked when he felt his own breath leaving him as Jack squeezed tighter. His third desperate blow made a crunching sound, and he felt something give way under his fists. Jack's grip loosened, and the small boy fell to the ground as Jack cried out and brought both hands to his broken nose.

Blood squeezed through the larger boy's fingers, and Owen quickly began looking for some other place on Jack's body to mount an attack. He put his hands together in a double fist again and hit Jack between *the legs with every bit of strength he had. Jack screamed and doubled over, holding his groin. He stumbled over the foot of Ansel's bed and landed on his side in the center aisle of the room. Owen rushed over and attacked Jack's unprotected face with both fists landing hard blows to the rapidly swelling bridge of Jack's nose.*

By now all the boys in the room were awake and watching the small boy's arms flailing like a threshing machine. Then one of the older boys got out of his bunk and grabbed the small attacker. He spoke softly to Owen. "That's enough! Let's not wake the brothers!" He led the smaller boy back to his bunk while the others picked Jack up off the floor.

Owen lay still in his bunk, his eyes wide, his breath coming fast in the dim light, not knowing what would happen next; when he realized nothing would, he relaxed and then felt satisfaction when he heard Jack sobbing softly in the same way Jack had made the smaller boys sob. He lay in his bunk and felt the dull ache of his hands and the sting on his cheek, but inside, he felt good. It was a clean, honest feeling. He thought that it might be the feeling the brothers told the boys they were supposed to have after receiving Holy Communion. But although he had received the Holy Sacrament regularly since his First Communion, he had never felt this good.

The next morning the brothers gathered all the boys in the dining hall. The boys stood at attention in a straight row, lined up according to age, youngest boy on one end, oldest on the other. Brother Xavier stood in front of the older boys, and two of his assistants stood at each end of the row. The brothers appeared stiff in their white collars and black frocks, and they all looked as if they had just caught the boys in an act of mortal sin.

"Well then. Who will tell me what happened?" Brother Xavier addressed the older boys.

The boys stared straight ahead in their silence. Brother Xavier walked over to Jack.

"*Let me be more specific. Who did this damage to Master Dupree's face?*" He glared at Jack.

The silence was complete. Not even the fearful breathing of the boys could be heard. Brother Xavier was a large man with a badly scarred face and only one eye.

"*Every one of you know that it is a mortal sin to tell a lie. It is also a sin to not speak the truth when it is known.*" *Brother Xavier walked back and forth in front of the older boys.* "*So, even if you do not lie to me but hide the truth, you will just as surely be damned to hell the same as if you lied.*" *His voice became much louder.* "*Now, who did this?*"

The older boys cringed at Brother Xavier's rage but remained silent. The small boy with the sore hands was giving some thought to the brother's words and had to agree with him on the point about mortal sin. It made sense to him that hiding the truth was the same as a lie, and if it was the same kind of sin, then it seemed only fair that you should receive the same kind of punishment. He struggled with this thought, trying to imagine what eternal damnation would be like. An image of large, blistering fires and the devil tormenting the suffering souls of hell formed bright and clear in his mind, and although he could not quite grasp the concept of eternity, he knew it was a very long time. He thought about it a while longer, and when there was no doubt left in him, he said, "*I did it, Brother Xavier.*" *He felt confident that any punishment the brothers handed out would be easier to suffer than eternal damnation and the fires of hell.*

"*What?*" *Brother Xavier appeared startled and walked down to the other end of the line.*

"*I said I did it, Brother Xavier, but I ain't sorry.*"

Brother Xavier reached out and squeezed the boy's left ear. "*Ain't, Master Jones?*"

"*I meant to say that I am not sorry I did it.*" *The older boys looked at Jack and giggled.*

"*Silence!*" *Brother Xavier leaned down and came face to face with the small boy. The scars that ran across the brother's red face looked blue in the cold light of the dining room. Owen tried not to look at the hole where the missing eye had once been.* "*You caused this devastation to Master Dupree's face?*"

"*Yes, Brother Xavier.*"

"*He did not!*" *Jack yelled out. All the boys laughed.*

"*Well now.*" *Brother Xavier grinned, and Owen looked away as the empty socket of the missing eye squeezed shut.* "*I wonder who is telling the truth and who is tempting the fires of hell?*" *He reached down and gently took the small boy's hands in his, inspecting them closely as he turned them over and then looked at the fresh abrasions on his cheek. He nodded to the other brothers, and they went down the line, carefully examining the hands of each boy. When they finished, they stepped back; each shook his head in Brother Xavier's direction.*

"*Now then, Master Dupree. You have a chance to reconsider, because unless St. Michael himself entered the dormitory last night, the only scars of battle are on you and ...*" *He turned and looked at the small boy, this young warrior. Would you care to tell me who did it?*"

Giggling and laughter broke out among all the boys. "*Silence, or there will be no breakfast!*" *Brother Xavier roared.*

Jack's eyes turned away from the brother, and his face turned a bright red.

"*I am waiting, Master Dupree! No details. I want a simple yes or no. Is this young man telling the truth?*"

"*Yes, but—*"

"*That will be all,*" *Brother Xavier said softly. He turned and walked slowly down the line of boys. The small boy noticed that the brother was still smiling. Without breaking his stride, and looking straight ahead, the brother said,* "*Stations of the Cross instead of supper tonight. You are dismissed.*"

Later, after breakfast, Owen went over to talk to Ansel, but Ansel refused to even look at him. During the next few weeks, Ansel withdrew more and more into himself, and every day the fear grew in his eyes. Ansel had a look that reminded Owen of the paintings he had seen of Christians in front of the lions in the Roman coliseum. He thought that it must be even worse than eternal damnation to carry around that much fear. Then one day, without any notice or announcement, Ansel was gone from the home. None of the boys knew where he had gone, but Owen hoped that it was to a place where he would not be afraid.

ONE

The lawman sat on his bedroll with his back against several large canvas sacks stacked behind him, his legs flat on the wooden floorboard of the Southern Pacific Express car. Precious Pete sat on the floor opposite him, with a hopeful smile on his face. The lawman noticed that when Pete began to smile there was something contagious about it. It made a person want to smile with him. Pete's eyebrows lifted in the middle and his blue eyes sparkled, lighting up his handsome face. But when his full lips pulled up and back, his front teeth became the prominent feature of his face, and what teeth were not missing were yellow and stained brown from well-water minerals. Stained teeth were not uncommon in Arizona Territory, but it was the greenish, moss-like matter hanging between the teeth at Pete's gumline that killed any contagious desire to smile with him.

In his forty-nine years of life, the lawman had seen men in all their shame and glory, but somehow, the spectacle of Pete's teeth was more than he could handle, and he turned to look out the open door of the car. He fought the drowsiness brought on by the rhythm of the steel wheels rolling over the joints in the rails and had caught himself nodding off several times since the train had pulled out of Tucson station. The lack of sleep during the chase and capture of Precious Pete had begun to take its toll.

Earlier, the railroad agent had brought him a sugared coffee from the dining car in a delicate white China cup, and this had revived him for a while. He was not worried about Precious Pete jumping him, for Pete was secured with eight pounds of chain that was girdled around his waist. The chain ran down between his legs to a double wrap on his ankles, where it was secured with a padlock. It then ran a few feet across the floor, around the leg of a half-ton railroad safe, and back through the wrap at Pete's waist to his wrists, where it took three tight turns and was padlocked again. Whenever Pete moved his hands or feet, the chain made a loud rattling sound as it moved along the wood floor and around the steel leg of the safe.

The lawman was taking Pete to Yuma Territorial Prison, where he would be held for the sheriff in Yuma County, who had the responsibility for Pete's execution. The railroad agent, in full defiance of the rules and regulations of Southern Pacific, had slid open the mail car door, and the dry breeze created by the speed of the train flowed into the car and eased the oven-like heat of the Arizona desert. Coal smoke and cinders occasionally swept into the car, but that was a small price to pay for the breeze. The lawman watched the dry landscape flow by as the train headed west across the bottom of the territory; he could see the vague humps of dark blue mountains to the south as they floated above the heat rising from the desert floor.

"How long you reckon it'll be?" Pete asked.

"About two hours, give or take."

"No. I mean how long before they hang me?"

The lawman looked back at Pete. "Don't know, Pete. That'll be up to the sheriff in Yuma."

Pete quit smiling and stared at the far wall of the car. "I never done nothin' to hurt nobody!" His voice took on a sullen tone.

The lawman glanced back at Pete, shook his head, and then returned his gaze to the open door.

"It was the others done all the shootin'. I just helped move the cattle."

"Not what the hands said."

"Lyin' bastards!"

"And the rancher's wife and the boy up on the Verde?"

"You know damn well that weren't me! I was over in St. Johns, nowheres near the Verde! It was the Breed done that! I done some bad things, but none like that!"

The lawman reached for his saddlebag, pulled it close, and took out a fresh plug of tobacco. He drew his knife from its scabbard and began to cut off a corner of the plug.

"I offered to testify on that one!"

"Yes, and I told the judge that, but he needs an eyewitness, not hearsay, and you didn't help yourself none when you broke out of jail in Benson and we had to run you to ground. No, Pete, it would take a lot more than good testimony to even things out."

Pete went quiet. He was thinking hard. The lawman got to his feet, caught his balance on the rocking floor of the express car and took the cut of tobacco over to his prisoner. Pete put the tightly packed tobacco in his mouth and began to chew slowly. He looked at the lawman and tried to think of a way out of this situation and his impending date with the hangman in Yuma. All because a dumb cowhand on a sorry excuse for a ranch in Yuma County tried to stop him stealing a few head of scrawny cows. He should have never stopped in Benson for a drink. He should have kept riding east, all the way to El Paso.

"What if I was to tell you about something you don't know 'bout yet?"

The lawman pushed his back up against the mail sacks and cut another piece off the plug. "What do you mean, Pete?" He put the tobacco in his mouth and began to chew slowly. He felt the saliva begin to flow, and the strong taste of the blocked leaf formed in his mouth, bringing alertness to his tired body and numbed mind.

"I mean I know what happened to the MacDuff women!"

The lawman put on a disinterested face. "There's talk about them runnin' off to her kin in Texas."

Pete looked at the lawman, disappointment on his face, but he recovered quickly. "That ain't what happened!" Pete began to smile again.

The lawman looked away, grabbed an empty fruit can on the floor next to the mail sacks, and threw it over to Pete. Pete grabbed it and dribbled a long stream of brown juice from his mouth to the can.

"That ain't what happened! If I was to tell you what happened, you reckon they would just keep me in prison 'stead of hanging me?"

"Don't know, Pete. I'd have to wire the judge. But I can tell you this for certain. I can't wire him with a promise; I'll need the facts as you know them, and then we'll see. I ain't lyin' to you, it's a gamble."

"You been real decent to me like no lawman I ever knew. You done shared your chew with me and all, but I got somethin' to trade and I don't trust no judge if I tell all before I get a deal!"

"Pete, I treated you like I did because, well hell, if you hadn't taken a couple of bad turns in life, who knows how things would have turned out."

What he did not tell Pete was that his actions were also in line with his captain's orders. Shortly after the captain was sworn in, he had drawn up six General Orders to help guide the actions of his men. Order number five stated: "A prisoner must be shown the courtesy due an unfortunate and the kindness a helpless man deserves and gets from a brave officer." There was something else in the order about showing the greatest humanity and putting yourself in the prisoner's place. High-minded ideas mostly, and good ones, he had to admit, but the lawman treated his prisoners decently because it was practical. This was hard country and these were hard men, but he had learned that most of them relaxed when treated with even a small amount of kindness, and when they relaxed, they talked. The lawman was not a particularly kind man, but he had obtained confessions from many a prisoner, and they would give him information about people and crimes in the territory simply because he treated them decently. Over time, these bits of information added up and gave him a leg up on criminal activity in the territory. When a man was on his way to the gallows, he had only the memories of his miserable life and a small amount of dignity left over from the time he was a free man. No need to take that away when the law was about to take his life. He had dealt with many men like Pete: young hellions full of fire and anxious to make a reputation. They were not real fighters, just killers with blown-up monikers who would rather back shoot a man or terrify women, but more often than not surrendered or tried to run when they met a man who would stand and fight. They were men of limited abilities and even more limited consciences. Pete was one of them. He was a liar, a coward, and a killer, but if he could help solve a crime and identify the criminals responsible, then the few hours between here and Yuma would credit him with more decency than most of his short, violent life had so far.

The train rattled on. The lawman was quiet. Pete was close to telling him something about the MacDuff women, so he intended to give him plenty of room. About five months ago, the MacDuff rig had been found abandoned on a road between their ranch and the Arizona town of Naco. It was a small town directly across the international border from its Mexican twin, also named Naco. Tracks had been found in the area, but no bodies, blood, or sign of a struggle. The rig was empty and the horse was gone. The lawman had followed the tracks for about a mile toward Naco, where they split into two groups and spread out on different paths to the border. He and his partner had counted twelve horses, including the MacDuff buggy horse. He remembered looking south where Arizona fell off gradually toward Mexico. The small border town of Naco stood out on the brush-covered slope. He had sat his horse for a long time as he looked south and considered the terror of a mother and her young daughter, helpless in the hands of a gang of cutthroat bandits. He had hoped they would receive some word of ransom for the women, but after several months with no contact, he was convinced that the women were dead and he would not allow himself to speculate on how they had met their end.

The lawman chewed slowly and spit into a spittoon next to the railroad agent's desk.

"I'll tell you what I know, but you gotta promise to wire the judge!"

"We'll see."

"Promise?"

"Now Pete, I can't promise 'til I know the facts. The judge'd have my hide if I was to wire him with no facts."

"All right, then! It was the Breed and his boys."

The lawman looked into Pete's eyes and waited. Pete was nervous and he looked away, not meeting the lawman's eyes.

"Hell, Pete. The judge would laugh me out of the territory if I went to him with that." He leaned back against the mail sacks, and just before he closed his eyes, he was surprised to see Pete's lower lip tremble just a bit. Now maybe it would come.

"We was ridin' to the border after selling off a herd to some men over on the Mogollon. We was ridin' hard, staying close to New Mexico most of the way. Spence said he had some business in Naco and said he would join us later in Mexico. We had plans to all meet on the Rio Sonora north of Bacoachic, where it takes a sharp turn to the west. We ran across the women on the road north of Naco, and the Breed, he got all excited, the mother bein' a real pretty blond and all. Some of the others was lickin' their chops too, but Spence wanted to just ride on. The Breed convinced him that we could ransom the women from the Mexican side of the border. 'Sides, they'd seen us and we was tryin' to get into Mexico without nobody knowin' where we was. After arguin' for a while, Spence agrees that the Breed had a good idea so we just unhitched the horse, lifted the women and their picnic basket, and headed south. After a little ways, we split into two bunches to go 'round Naco. Spence, he tells me to ride with the Breed, who got the women, and make sure he don't hurt them. We made good time and was far into Mexico before dark. We made dry camp that night and 'cept for tyin' them up, the women wasn't hurt none. The mother, she was real proud and she stared the Breed down a couple o' times. The girl was real scared and she cried, quiet like, all the time. The next day we headed out to the meeting place on the Rio Sonora. We got there just after noon and set up camp close to the river and waited for Spence." Pete stopped talking and was quiet for a while. He looked off into the middle distance. "We ate their picnic lunch that was in the basket."

"How old was the girl, Pete?" The lawman's voice was soft.

Pete looked at him and then quickly turned his eyes back to the middle distance. "I don't know."

"Take a guess." The lawman's voice was still soft.

"I said I don't know!"

"She just turned ten years old, Pete." His voice was just a bit harder now.

"Well, I didn't have nothin' to do with her, dammit!" Pete stopped and spit more tobacco juice into the can. He looked at the lawman, hoping that he would not have to go on.

"This man you call the Breed. Is he the one goes by the name of Joaquin Mitchell?" the lawman asked.

"Yeah, that's him." Pete smiled again. He was being helpful.

"'Bout five foot nine, real dark, barrel chest, black hair? The one robbed the bank in Winslow?"

"That's him. He got green eyes. And somethin' else. His feet, he got web feet like a duck."

"How do you mean, Pete?"

"His toes got this skin between 'em. All of 'em. In that village—down on the Yaqui—they call him El Pato Prieto. He hates bein' called a duck. I seen him stab a fella called him that."

"Do you reckon he'd run down to that village. Lay low down in Sonora?"

"Nah! His folks is dead and he lets everyone know he hates his kin. 'Sides, he claims he killed his father down in that village. I don't think he'd go back."

The lawman knew Mitchell well. The year before, Mitchell and a gang had robbed the bank in Winslow, and as he and the gang rode out of town, he shot two citizens who were standing outside a café minding their own business. The sheriff and his posse caught up with the gang the next day, and after a shootout in which two of the gang were killed, Mitchell surrendered. A mob of citizens had formed in town and demanded the sheriff hand Mitchell over so they could hang him from a telegraph pole. The sheriff talked the mob down and convinced them to go

home. The next morning Mitchell killed a deputy who was escorting him to the toilet and escaped. The sheriff later told the
lawman: "I wish I had let those people have the no-good son of a
bitch. He'd be dead and my deputy would still be alive."

They were silent for a while. The lawman was making mental
notes, and Pete was reliving the crime-filled day, hoping that he
would not have to tell any more. The lawman leaned forward and
looked Pete in the eye.

"What happened next?"

Pete looked like he had been betrayed and was quiet for a moment as if deciding whether he should continue. The lawman was
patient but had a determined look on his face. Pete looked down
at the fruit can between his legs and spoke in a subdued voice.

"We waited for Spence. I was surely hopin' he would get there
soon, but it weren't to be. The Breed and the boys was drinkin'
and playin' cards most of the afternoon and then they started
payin' a lot more 'tention to the women. They …" Pete broke off
and stared down at the can.

The lawman could see that Pete was truly in agony, and he
wanted to give Pete plenty of time, but after a while, it was apparent that he needed coaxing. "Go on, Pete." His voice was soft and
encouraging.

Pete avoided the lawman's eyes.

"They took turns with the woman and then, they … I want
you to know I didn't have nothin' to do with the girl! I swear on
my mother's grave!"

"I know, Pete. I never figured you for that kind of man." The
lawman's voice was still soft and reassuring, but he felt the rage
building in him as the truth of the women's fate began to take
shape in the hot express car. How could this cowardly little bastard swear on his mother's grave? He fought hard to control the
rage. He wanted to keep Pete talking.

"When they was through with the woman, the Breed cut her throat, and then they went over to get the girl." Tears ran down Pete's handsome face, and for a moment, it appeared that he might just start to blubber.

"And?" the lawman prodded.

"Well, they raped her!"

"Who raped the girl, Pete?"

"The Breed and Zeke Bent!"

"Who killed her?"

"The Breed."

"Cut her throat?"

"No!" Pete broke off with a choked sob. Tears ran freely down his face, and tobacco juice leaked out of his mouth, forming small bubbles of brown foam at the corners of his full lips.

The lawman let Pete seep in the misery of his memories for a while longer and then in a quiet voice said, "Go on."

"He, he picked her up by her feet, she was just a teeny little thing. From where I was standin', she looked like a little china doll, all white and crying for her mama. And there was blood all over her, you know, from when they ..." Pete was quiet again.

The lawman said nothing but took some satisfaction in the depth of Pete's agonies.

"And then he swung her down, smashing her on the ground like you would a gut-shot rabbit. Then he did it again and then she didn't make no more noise."

Pete was just about wrung out, and the lawman knew he would hold nothing back now. "Did you rape Mrs. McDuff?"

"Yes." Pete spoke in a monotone. "God help me, I did!"

"Did you tell me all this in hopes you wouldn't hang, or did you tell me to clear your conscience?"

Pete looked up, and the lawman thought that if Pete had ever in his life had a moment of honesty, this was it.

"I started out tellin' you to save my neck, but after I started, I reckon, well, I reckon I just wanted to make a clean breast of it all."

"Who else raped Mrs. MacDuff?"

"An old guy name of Harvey Miller. He stays drunk most of the time. Ezekiel Bent and a Mexican called Mocho. That Ezekiel is just as bad as the Breed, worse in some ways. I'm pretty sure it was him done the woman and boy up on the Verde. He likes hurtin' people."

"Where can I find them?"

"Last I seen 'em, they was still with the Breed in Mexico."

"Now tell me, what did you do with the bodies?"

"Some of the boys that didn't have nothin' to do with it, well, the Breed made them dig a deep hole and put the bodies in and cover them up."

"Where?"

"On the east bank between the river and a stand of old cottonwoods."

"Who are these boys and where can I find them?"

"Johnny Richardson and Octavio Paz, a couple of ranch hands from the Verde spread who fell in with us when we rustled that herd. Don't know where they are now. Next mornin', they was just gone."

"Now tell me about this Spence, is that his first name or last?"

"That's the only name I know him by. He's tall, has long dark hair and a beard. Got a scar above his eyes. He's smart. Real quiet. Supposed to have went to some fancy school back East. He kept to hisself mostly, but he paid good and I woulda rode with him again if I had a chance, but after Naco, I never saw him again. He never made the meeting place, so me and the boys drifted south. I stayed there a couple of months until I got tired of Mexico and Mexicans, and then came back to the territory. That's all I know."

"Where does the gang hide out in Sonora?"

"They stay in the high country, like the 'Paches used to, but the Breed, he likes to be close to towns so he can get mescal and supplies. We would ride into them little Mexican towns and just get what we needed. They never had much, just some corn and beans and aguardiente."

"Was he still in touch with Spence?"

"Don't know. Him and Spence, they never told us much 'bout their plans—only what we was gonna do and when we was gonna do it. I did hear that the Breed was supposed to go to Hermosillo to meet someone. I figured it to be Spence, but that's 'bout the time I left."

They were both quiet, each lost in thought. Pete slowly chewed tobacco and stared at the wall of the car across from him. The lawman looked out the door at the passing desert, losing track of time until the Southern Pacific agent came into the car and began pulling the door closed.

"Just twenty miles to Yuma." he announced.

The lawman took an oilskin pouch from his saddlebags, opened it, and removed several sheets of foolscap and a pencil. As the train slowed during its approach to Yuma, he sat at the railroad agent's desk and began to write. He wrote quickly what he had already composed in his mind, and by the time the train stopped at the station, he had completed his work.

The prison wagon was waiting on the far side of the baggage room. The lawman checked in with the stationmaster for messages and then arranged for the unloading of his tack. He then led Pete, still in chains, across the wooden platform and down the ramp to the prison wagon.

The guard at the main gate of Yuma Territorial Prison watched the prison wagon make its way around the corner and up the main road that ran along the river in front of the prison. The wagon stopped fifty yards east of the gate, in accordance with prison regulations, and the prisoner was removed at that spot. The guard watched as the lawman and the prisoner walked slowly up the hill toward him. A stiff breeze blew in off the river and stirred up clouds of dust that rolled low over the road so that the two men appeared to float above the hard-packed dirt. Except for the fact that one man was in chains, there was not much difference in the appearance of the two men. They were both covered with dust and looked like tired cowhands coming in after a long trail drive. They were dressed in frayed and worn clothing, but as they came nearer, the guard noticed that the lawman was at least clean-shaven. He noticed something else, too. The lawman, although moving like he was dog-tired, explored his surroundings with his eyes, his head swiveling from side to side, constantly moving and taking in everything around him.

After asking for the officer of the watch, the lawman took his prisoner to a spot under the awning at the front gate and waited. The guard called for his sergeant and then lounged in the shade of a small building attached to the front wall of the prison.

Pete was bent over, as if the chains were pulling him to the ground. He appeared to be resigned to his fate. The mud-colored walls of the prison rose high above him, and he realized his chances for freedom were gone forever.

"I'd rather they shoot me than hang me," Pete said to no one in particular.

"I don't think you have any selection in the matter, Pete." The lawman looked up at the brown walls. The guard laughed.

"Well, I sure wish I knew how long it'll be." Pete was looking at the huge wooden and metal gates in front of him.

The guard laughed again and said, "They'll keep you here long enough for you to get used to the heat so's to prepare you for your long stay in hell, then they'll hang you."

The lawman turned to the guard and gave him a cold look that iced over the disgust he felt at the guard's remark. In a voice just loud enough for the guard to hear, he said, "Will you please check with the officer about the transport party?"

The guard broke away from the lawman's glare and went into the small building.

The lawman turned back to Pete. "Pete, I have written up a statement that I want you to look over, and if you agree with it, I want you to sign it."

"I, I can't read," Pete said.

The gate creaked on its hinges as it swung open, and a sergeant and two guards came forward to meet them. They took Pete and the lawman inside through the gate and walked over to a small building. The lawman removed the chains from Pete's body; when he was finished, the guards shackled the hands and feet of their new prisoner.

"Sergeant, I would appreciate it if you would serve as a witness to an official statement." The lawman was putting the chains into a canvas bag.

"I can do that, but I'd like to get the transfer orders and our paperwork done first."

The lawman nodded and waited while the sergeant filled in the blanks and signed the prison paperwork. He then gave the sergeant a small canvas sack containing Pete's personal items.

"Pete, I wrote down what you told me on the train. I'm going to read it to you, and if you agree with it, and only if you agree, I want you to sign it."

Pete nodded his head.

The lawman began to read. "I, Samuel Jens Petersen, also known as Pete Petersen and Precious Pete, give this statement freely and of my own will. I do so without any promises being made to me and under no duress."

Pete interrupted. "Duress?"

"It means I didn't threaten you in any way, Pete." Pete nodded his head.

The lawman continued, "In February of this year I was with the gang that took Mrs. MacDuff and her daughter from their buggy north of Naco, Arizona Territory, and transported them to Sonora, Mexico, where we planned to ransom them back to their family. The head of the gang was a man known to me only as Spence. We split into two groups; Spence went into Naco, and the rest of us went to Mexico. On the Rio Sonora north of Bacoachic, we raped and murdered Mrs. MacDuff. Joaquin Mitchell, myself, Harvey Miller, Ezekiel Bent, and a Mexican known to me as Mocho raped Mrs. MacDuff. Mitchell then killed her by cutting her throat. Mitchell and Bent then raped Mrs. MacDuff's daughter, Susan, and Mitchell killed her by slamming her body to the ground. Johnny Richardson and Octavio Paz, who did not take part in either rape, buried Mrs. MacDuff and her daughter on the east bank of the Rio Sonora under a stand of cottonwoods where the river makes a sharp westward bend north of Bacoachic. Signed and sworn on this twenty-ninth day of September, 1908."

The sergeant looked at Pete and shook his head in disgust.

"Sound about right, Pete?"

"'Zactly as I told you, but—that part about no promises—I mean—ain't you going to wire the judge?"

The lawman looked at Pete and let the silence take a strong hold.

"Do you still really want me to, Pete?" His voice was soft, confiding.

Pete stared at the floor, tears in his eyes. "No. I don't reckon it'll do me any good now. But I been thinkin' on this, and there is one promise I want before I make my mark."

"What's that, Pete?"

"I got a daughter in Tucson. Her name is Sara and she's two years old. Her mother is Janie Shaw. She worked over at the Palace Saloon the last I knew. I ain't seen them in a while. There's a five-dollar gold piece and a ring, belonged to my mother, there in that sack on the table. I want you to promise you'll give it to Sara." Tears welled up in Pete's eyes.

"All right, then, Pete, I promise I'll do that."

The lawman put the statement on the table next to the canvas sack. "Now, if you'll put your mark here, the sergeant and I will witness it." He gave Pete a pencil and showed him where to sign. Pete swung the chains from the hand shackles out of the way and made a scribbled "S J P" at the bottom of the single sheet of paper.

"I just want you to know, I, I ..." Pete shook his head. Sweat ran down his face, stinging his eyes, and he squeezed them shut. A sense of desperation suddenly came over him, and he felt the need to tell the lawman something, anything. He did not know for sure what he wanted to say, he searched for words that the lawman might take away with him, but after a moment, when he could find nothing in the rush of thoughts that ran through his mind, he stood still and quiet.

The lawman said nothing, and when Pete opened his eyes and looked at him, he felt a small shock go through him. The lawman's eyes were cold and hard, and he looked right through Pete. It was as if Pete no longer existed. It was if they had never met and the lawman was a thousand miles away.

The sergeant leaned over the table and signed Pete's statement. He wrote his name out slowly: Zachary Wills, Sgt., Yuma Territorial Prison. The lawman signed at the very bottom of the page: Owen P. Jones, Arizona Ranger, Arizona Territory.

TWO

————◆————

The man known as Spence leaned back against a leather seat embossed with the words *Ferrocarril de Mexico* and puffed lightly on a cigar. Maybe it was his imagination, but the Mexican trains seemed to run with less noise and with more comfort than those in the United States. The businessman across from him was reading the Mexican newspaper *La constitución*, whose front page proclaimed another oil strike near Tampico. A photo of President Porfirio Díaz meeting with some foreign diplomats in a formal setting at Chapultepec castle dominated the page above the fold; the lower right corner had a small article about unrest among the peasants in the state of Morelos. Yet another article announced that a politico named Madero would challenge Díaz in the national elections. Spence put all of this together with what he had learned from his sources in Mexico about a conflict between Díaz and some políticos in Chihuahua and began to have real concerns about the stability of the Díaz regime.

He shot the cuffs of his boiled shirt and brushed stray ash from the sleeve of his worsted suit. He admired the stiff French cuffs and the gold cufflinks, which, along with the pearl stickpin in his tie, were small concessions he made to the sober and formal dress of a businessman in the Republic of Mexico. He puffed slowly on the cigar and thought about the articles on the front page of the newspaper. Even though the Porfiriato was at its peak of success and Mexico had never been more prosperous, his friends in Mexico City were not optimistic about the future. They told him that change was in the wind, and the general consensus was that the change would be drastic. This concerned him because he knew that in Mexico even a slight threat to the stability of the regime could cause a large increase in security; and his scheme depended on less security, not more.

The businessman across from Spence put down his newspaper and leaned his head back against the soft leather. In a few minutes, he was snoring softly.

It wasn't just Mexico where the status quo was threatened, Spence thought. Things were changing all over the world, and the pace of change seemed to have quickened with Queen Victoria's death back in '01. The real trick was to be on top of it, to anticipate the possibilities and explore the new potential that change would bring about. He could still build on his experience of the past, but it was the anticipation of the unexplored that would test him, and he did not lack confidence in his ability to trump any new challenge he would face. Thinking about his new schemes made his latest adventures in Arizona seem so elementary.

Cattle rustling, although not his first choice for making money, had been easy, and Spence's tight management of planning and operations had given him a modest return on his investment. It had also given him a chance to disappear for a while into the vastness of Arizona Territory. His only two ventures in rustling had been meticulously planned and executed because he had provided hands-on oversight and had sold the cattle even before undertaking each operation. His problem had been in finding experienced cowhands who could move large herds of stolen cattle to the buyers. He had been forced to employ some marginal hands from the gutters and saloons of Arizona and New Mexico. Mitchell and his crew were perfect examples. It frustrated Spence to no end that they were constantly distracted from their work by the appearance of anyone they considered an easy target. These distractions could be the easy pickings of a traveling businessman with a few dollars in his pocket, the sparse pickings from a remote farm, and especially the presence of any female. Rape and murder came easy to these men because they were not smart enough to think beyond the next meal or bottle of whiskey. He was not opposed to violence. In fact, his plans sometimes required it, but beyond that, he considered it a waste of time and effort.

Before Arizona, he had come close to disaster in the Midwest when a scheme failed miserably and his identification with this scheme had forced him to lie low and search for other possibilities. Oregon and the Northwest held nothing but small farms and towns with no prospects for any of his plans. California held a lot of wealth but was being settled and organized so that freewheeling actors like him did not fit in. The big money of the corporations and railroads controlled most of the state, forcing freelancers to fight for the crumbs. Now Arizona and New Mexico were scrambling for statehood, trying to prove to the world that they were civilized, and the days of wild Indians and Billy the Kid were dead and gone.

Mexico had always attracted him, and he had traveled extensively throughout the republic, making valuable contacts and establishing a reputation in banking and financial circles. The political and financial state of the republic was perfect for several schemes he had in mind. So, with some trusted colleagues, he had put together a project that promised a healthy return on investment.

Spence put out his cigar and decided to make his way to the dining car for a late breakfast. The train was scheduled to arrive in Hermosillo at four o'clock that afternoon, and he did not want a heavy lunch sitting on his stomach for the rest of the trip.

There was only one vacant table in the dining car, and the waiter, with his black jacket and tie and ankle-length boiled white apron, escorted him to it. Spence ordered, in Spanish, coddled eggs and toast and admired the burnished walnut and polished brass in the car while the waiter poured the coffee. He sipped his coffee and looked out the window at the peasants and their donkeys working the small green plots they called milpas. He thought he could see the dark outline of the Sierra Madre off to the east but then thought that it could just be the gathering of clouds for the September rains. Then his mind wandered to Hermosillo and his planned meeting with one Señor Silva at the Banco del Mar. He was content when he thought of his account there as well as the one in Mexico City. His second meeting would be with an old colleague with whom he had worked several complicated bond swindles in the past. One of these schemes had been very lucrative, and the other a near disaster that had them leaving Chicago one step ahead of the Pinkertons.

Spence was sipping at his coffee, reliving the excitement of his close escape, when he saw her enter the dining car. She was with an older man, and their dress confirmed in his mind that they were definitely upper class. She was a striking young woman. He had to force himself to look away so as not to offend the Mexican sense of propriety. He looked out the window, but out of the corner of his eye, he saw the waiter approach his table.

"Pardon, señor." The waiter lifted his eyebrows and looked at the couple.

"Of course!" Spence replied, standing as the waiter pulled back a chair on the opposite side of the table for the woman. My God!

She's even more beautiful up close, he thought. He remained standing and met the eye of the man, then held out his hand.

"John Stanford," he announced, shaking hands with the man.

"Nicolás del Castillo," the man replied. He had a dry and firm handshake. "My wife, Eugenia." He put his hand on her shoulder.

"A pleasure," Spence said. "Please sit down." He addressed them in formal Spanish.

They placed their order with the waiter, and the man sat with his hands folded on the edge of the table. "You have excellent Spanish, Mr. Stanford." The man studied his business attire.

"Your English is equally excellent, Señor del Castillo." Spence maintained eye contact with the man, willing himself not to look at the woman.

"It appears that everyone on the train is on our dining schedule," the woman said. Her voice was clear with a cultured tone. She sat with her hands in her lap, her back straight as she glanced around the dining car. The men smiled politely at her observation. The waiter brought the eggs and toast and set them on the table before Spence.

"Please, Mr. Stanford, do not wait. We have intruded on you sufficiently, and we cannot allow the suffering of a cold breakfast." The man smiled.

Spence nodded his appreciation and picked up a spoon. They engaged in polite conversation, discussing the state of the railroad in Mexico, talking about restaurants in the capital, and making general observations about the state of the economy.

The woman was quiet, letting the men talk for a while, before breaking all convention when she asked, "Are you in business in Mexico, Mr. Stanford?"

Her husband raised his eyebrows just slightly in reaction to this breach of social decorum.

"I am an investment banker from San Francisco, and my clients have interests in mining and oil throughout the republic." Spence placed one of his cards on the table in front of del Castillo. It was embossed discreetly in gold-lettering with his name and an address on Market Street in San Francisco, California.

When the woman looked up from his card, Spence could have reached over and picked out the large gold flecks in the light green of her eyes.

"Were you there during the earthquake?"

"No. Fortunately, business had taken me to New York, but our building was destroyed, along with a great deal of our records. In fact, I am in Mexico still trying to locate some of our duplicate records."

"Will you be in Hermosillo long?" Her eyes looked directly at him.

Her husband was now obviously put out by her questioning and abruptly directed the conversation back to general talk of Mexico City and other matters. They talked on in short, polite sentences.

The woman was silent again, but she studied John Stanford's face. She noted that his hair was neatly groomed. It was short and black, and it shone without the benefit of the pomade that was so popular but that she found distasteful. He had laughing blue eyes and clear skin. His nose was small and straight and there was a distinctive scar that ran through one eyebrow. He had a mustache in the Mexican style, not bushy but neatly trimmed, and it set off his perfectly white and straight teeth. He spoke excellent Spanish, and she liked the way he addressed them in the formal manner and not in the rude, familiar way that so many of his countrymen used when they learned Spanish. She sensed that he was more than just a businessman from San Francisco, but whoever he was, she knew that he was definitely the most intriguing thing she had encountered on this otherwise tedious trip.

After finishing their breakfast, Señor del Castillo got up and stood behind his wife's chair. "Perhaps our paths will cross in Hermosillo," he said as he pulled back his wife's chair.

Not exactly an invitation, Spence thought. "I would welcome the opportunity." He stood and bowed slightly.

They nodded their goodbyes, and then the couple made their way to the end of the dining car. As her husband opened the door, the woman turned and smiled back at Spence's table. It was a smile that left no doubt.

Now that, he thought, is an invitation.

THREE

————◆————

The telegram was waiting for Jones at the hotel:
> *Come to Tucson soonest—Rustlers east territory—*
> *Capt. Wheeler*

Jones checked with the desk man and learned the next train to Tucson left at seven in the morning. He arranged to have his tack taken to the train depot and then looked forward to a bath, a steak, and a good night's sleep.

After his bath, Jones took a clean change of clothes out of his grip. He dressed and then dusted off his boots and hat and went down to the lobby. The sun was down behind the buildings across the street, causing the shadows to cross over and lie on the sidewalk in front of the hotel. Jones heard the bell of the trolley as it turned the corner down the street, and he felt things closing in on him as they always did when he was in town.

"Shine, señor?" A small boy holding a wooden box looked up at him.

"Where is Carlito?" he asked the boy in Spanish.

"Now he works for El Chino."

"At the *lavandería*?"

"Sí, señor."

"How much will you cost me?"

The boy smiled at the ranger's imperfect Spanish. "Veinte centavos!" he answered.

"Bueno!" The ranger sat on a bench in front of the hotel's plate-glass windows and practiced his Spanish on the boy. He was a serious boy and worked hard on the ranger's scuffed and worn boots. Jones learned that Carlito, who had been the hotel's unofficial bootblack, now worked for the Chinaman, picking up and delivering laundry on a bicycle. The boy thought it was a good job, but he told the ranger that he preferred the life of a bootblack.

"But surely Carlito can make more money with El Chino?" Jones asked the boy.

"Yes. At times. But if I work harder and faster, then I make more money than him. And more than that …" He stopped working the brush across the ranger's boots and smiled. "I am the boss!"

The boy finished his work and stood up. "You like?" he asked the ranger.

"Very much!" Jones reached into his pocket and pulled out a half dollar. "Do you have change?"

"No, señor."

"Can you have some?"

The boy knew it was rude, but he could not keep from correcting this man's Spanish. "Can you get some," the boy corrected in Spanish. And then, "Yes, I can get some!"

The boy took the silver coin. He looked at his box on the sidewalk and then looked up at the ranger. He stooped down quickly to pick up the box and put it under his arm; then he ran down the street to the corner, turned left and disappeared from sight.

Jones could see the last rays of sunlight flashing red and orange on the fading blue sky between the buildings and thought about

Mrs. MacDuff and her daughter. Without Pete's confession, their disappearance would have remained a mystery. As he recalled Pete's description of the crime, he felt his control slip a little. Killings were a fairly common occurrence in the territory, and he had seen his share. But if Pete was telling the truth, and there was no reason to doubt him, the killing of the MacDuff women was the type of outrage he had not seen in a long while. A drunk miner or ranch hand who shot or stabbed someone in a saloon was one thing, but this, along with the killing of the woman and boy up on the Verde, caused him real concern because he had not seen this kind of viciousness since he had rangered in far west Texas. He leaned back on the wooden bench and in the cooling twilight thought about Texas.

He had been part of a detachment of Company D, Texas Rangers, at Fort McKavett that was being sent to Fort Stockton and then on to Fort Davis to explore the need for a permanent Ranger base in the Big Bend country. At the time he enlisted in the Rangers, the Comanche raiding had been stopped all along the frontier and Quanah Parker and his people were confined to a reservation in northeast Texas and Oklahoma. But the Rangers still had bandits, train robbers, and rustlers to deal with, as well as a few small renegade groups of Apaches.

Sergeant Sutton, one of the old Comanche fighters, drove the Rangers hard on their way to Fort Stockton. On the fourth day, early in the morning, they saw a thin wisp of gray smoke on the far side of a long low hill about two miles to their front. The sergeant turned in his saddle and looked back at the sun. He then had the troop check their weapons and directed them slightly north and west so that they followed the rise of the hill and could make their approach from the high ground with the sun at their backs.

"If there is evil on the other side of that rise, then it's most likely already over. We'll ride in column to the top of the rise and then form line and ride down the other side." Sergeant Sutton took point and led them on their circuitous route to the hill.

As they came down off the rise, they could see three adobe buildings and a small corral. A buckboard was smoldering in the yard next to the largest of the buildings, and as they neared the small ranch, they could see what had happened. Jones had seen dead people before, those who had been hanged or shot or stabbed to death, but he was not prepared for the savagery that had been unleashed on this ranch family in far west Texas. Even several of the more experienced rangers were sickened at the sight of the butchery, but Sergeant Sutton appeared more curious than anything else. He instructed four of the troop to look through the buildings while he positioned the others for covering fire. After the buildings were cleared, he dismounted and examined each body very carefully, gently lifting a limb or turning a head to get a closer look. He took his time, and when he was finished, he called the troop together in front of the main building.

"John, I want you and Trey to go over and start figuring out their trail. Billy and Ira, y'all go through each building and find what personal effects you can and bring them to me. The rest of y'all will come with me and help give these poor folks a decent burial."

It was when they gathered up the bodies for burial that Jones was aware, for the first time, of a terrible anger burning in his chest. Only the physical task of burying the family prevented the immensity of this anger from overcoming him. He hated something, someone. He was not sure what or who, and this unfocused rage confused him.

A white man, a woman, and two small children lay in the center of the yard, and a Mexican male was tied with rope to a wagon wheel of the buckboard. They were all mutilated in such a way that their deaths must have been slow and horribly painful. At first he had felt fear, but this had quickly been replaced with the anger that screamed out for revenge, and when they picked up the bodies of the children, the fire of his rage made him fear for his sanity. He had always been quick to anger, but over the years, the anger had burned off almost as quickly as it began. This time he knew the rage would stay with him a long time.

After they had buried the family, Sergeant Sutton called them together at the main building. "Here's what we know. There's about a dozen of them, and four are riding shod ponies. Some of these shoes match tracks in the corral, but there are others that don't, so there might be some whites or Mexicans riding with this bunch. They're herding about four cows. The rancher was shot four times in the chest with a forty-four or forty-five, which makes me wonder again about white renegades, but the rest of it was pure Apache. We are going to give chase and bring this bunch to justice, so check your weapons, fill your canteens and the water bags, and grab a bite of biscuit and jerky, 'cause we ain't stopping until we find 'em."

The trail of the raiders led north and west into the Davis Mountains. The raiders were careless and did not appear to be in a hurry. The rangers came across remnants of women's clothing and other loot from the ranch as the trail climbed through the foothills. In the afternoon they found a butchered steer with only parts of the hindquarter missing. When the sergeant held up the steer's severed leg, fresh blood ran. He nodded grimly and remounted.

They found the raiders late that evening, camped in a valley by a small trickle of a stream. Sergeant Sutton broke his troop into two groups, one at each end of the valley, and they watched through the night, taking two-hour shifts. They planned the attack for first light; the sergeant would lead the main body from the higher ground at the south end of the valley, and Jones's group would cut the escape route at the north end.

As the morning light cracked the edge of the horizon, Sergeant Sutton and his group began their careful approach to the Indian camp and were within fifty yards when someone in the camp shouted out an alarm. The rangers broke into a gallop, riding straight for the Indians. It was not until they were close in that the reports from Colt revolvers could be heard by the rangers in Jones's group as they were lying prone behind cover with their Winchesters sighted down the sloping valley. Two Apaches rode out of the camp, and three more were fleeing on foot toward them. Jones and the corporal were to take the first of the raiders and lined up on the two who were horseback. They waited until the fleeing raiders were almost within handgun range and then fired their Winchesters. The thirty-caliber slugs knocked the braves off their horses. The Indians who were on foot stopped and tried to angle toward the streambed, but they were already in the sights of the other rangers and were quickly cut down.

Jones and the men mounted their horses and approached the camp in line from the north, moving slightly east to stay out of the line of fire. The sounds of more shooting and hollering reached them from the camp, but no other Indians tried to escape in their direction. After a few moments, the shooting stopped and the corporal hollered out for Sergeant Sutton. After making sure that all the rangers were accounted for, they quickened their approach to the camp. Jones, who was anchoring the end of the line closest to the stream bed, caught a flash of movement on his right. He brought his carbine to his shoulder and looked over the sights, trying to bring the movement into focus. Then he saw him. An Apache was running north on the far side of the stream and was about twenty-five yards from a large growth of salt cedar.

Jones tucked his cheek into the Winchester's stock and lined up his sights. He slowly swung the carbine to his right, leading the Indian slightly, holding at the front of his body. He squeezed the trigger, and the Apache was flung sideways and down.

The other rangers quickly came up and covered Jones as they looked for more runners. Jones and the corporal rode over to the fallen Indian. They crossed the stream, which at this point was almost dry, *and nudged their horses up the small incline to find the Indian lying in the broken shale of an old landslide. He was a young boy, and there was a large amount of blood pumping out of him. He looked up at the rangers, but the light was already fading from his eyes.*

"Looks like you hit the big artery," the corporal said. Jones dismounted and walked over to the dying boy. He had automatically chambered another round after his shot, and he held the carbine at the ready, covering the fallen boy, who watched him approach with a blank stare. Jones could see the boy's empty hands out in front of him, but he looked around for a weapon, all the same. As he got closer, he heard a sigh, and then, as he watched, the boy died, still looking at him. Jones walked a twenty-five-foot circle around the boy, searching for a weapon, but found nothing. He stood there, puzzled, and then he heard more pistol shots from the camp. He studied the dead boy for a moment and remounted and rode with the others into the camp, where Sergeant Sutton and his men were standing over several dead Indians and were reloading their Colts. The quiet that followed the savagery of their quick, violent action stayed with the men as they went about the business of searching the campsite and then securing their weapons and horses. There was not a word said for a long time, each man still tense and ready for action, each of them trying to recall how he had acted during the assault. After a while, they realized that there was not much memory except the noise of the weapons as they had concentrated on their targets. There had been thirteen men and young boys in the raiding party. There were no whites or Mexicans, as they had first suspected. Not one of the Indians survived the assault. The rangers had not suffered a single scratch.

The rangers left the Indians as they lay, and after gathering a few small personal effects of the rancher's family, they rode on to Fort Stockton. The fact that there were no women or small children with the raiders meant that this was strictly a raiding party, so there was probably a larger group of Apaches somewhere in the area, maybe more remnants of Victorio's old gang.

Jones felt the anger diminish, followed by a dull numbness. He thought about the boy he had killed and for a while dwelled on the fact that the boy had not been armed. He thought that he should feel bad about it, but he didn't.

After they rode into Fort Stockton, they set up camp behind the new Ranger quarters. As Jones was organizing his kit, Sergeant Sutton pulled him aside to tell him that the captain had ordered Sutton to ride over to Fort Davis with a detachment of three rangers. The sergeant wanted Jones to be one of them. They would ride out with fresh mounts first thing in the morning.

The sound of the steel wheels of the trolley on its track as it made its way slowly down the street grated on Jones's ears and interrupted his thoughts of Texas. He sat on the bench under the covered entrance to the hotel and enjoyed the absence of the heat as evening came on, and he thought about leaving Yuma in the morning. He glanced at the corner of the block where he had last seen the boy and then turned and watched the shadows grow longer in the dirt street. After a while, the boy turned the corner and ran up to him. The boy held out the change for the fifty-cent piece. The ranger gave him two dimes, which the boy put in his pocket. Jones looked at the rest of the change, tossing the coins in his hand a moment, and then looked down at the boy and handed him another dime and a nickel.

"Gracias, jefe!"

"Por nada," Jones replied, then began walking down the street. His polished boots were like strange appendages at the end of his legs, but he was satisfied with their shine and his mouth watered in anticipation of a steak, a side of potatoes, and a large slice of apple pie at the Acme Grille.

FOUR

he chief auditor was a fussy man. He was fussy about his work, his food, his appearance, and his comfort. Only the finest wool from England was fashioned into suits to fit his bulk by the best haberdashery shops in Manhattan. Once a week he had his hair and beard neatly trimmed and his nails finely manicured at the Luxor Tonsorial Parlor for Gentlemen on Fifth Avenue, three blocks from his office. He dined out seven days a week, at least two of those at the Palm Restaurant in the Waldorf. He was particularly fond of the Lobster Newberg and Beef Wellington, which he washed down with the finest wines from France. He allowed himself one cigar a day and always had it after dinner with a large snifter of Napoleon brandy. But what he truly enjoyed was sitting on the inside of the red rope at the Waldorf and watching the unfortunates on the other side of the velvet cord. It was a barrier that separated him from the others and told the world that he belonged and they did not. At one time the thought had crossed his mind that he should perhaps have some pity on them, but he couldn't find it in him and so thereafter never gave it another thought.

The maître d' knew him and was well aware of his important position as chief auditor and personal troubleshooter for the president of the Consolidated Mineral and Mining Corporation. He was pompous and could be overbearing, but the headwaiter had learned that if the auditor was treated as a swell by the staff and his habitual choices on the menu were consistently prepared in the manner he desired, he was always generous with the tip.

The chief auditor chewed carefully on the salad that was the specialty of the Waldorf and thought about work. He had a very large staff of accountants and bookkeepers, and he drove them hard. He personally selected each of the head accountants at the corporation's field locations around the world, and he maintained close contact to ensure that things were done in accordance with the president's wishes. His large salary, equally large bonuses, and thus his comfort depended on his ability to keep the numbers balanced and take care of problems before they came to the attention of the president. He took pride in his ability to nip problems in the bud, and the president relied on him to keep any unpleasantness as distant as possible from the front office.

That was why he was particularly concerned about the Mexican operation. He had not been able to put his finger on the problem, but the last two quarterly reports indicated weaknesses in numbers that should have shown stronger growth. It alarmed him even more that when he asked the head accountant in Mexico, a man named McLeod, for more complete data, the man had stalled and then furnished incomplete reports. He remembered McLeod as a steady, dependable fellow and a stickler for detail. But things just did not add up, and the chief auditor's instincts told him that McLeod required more attention. The dollar amount of the irregularities was significant enough for his personal attention, and that always meant personally conducting an on-site audit.

He had seen it happen before: an employee "went native" in a foreign country and engaged in minor schemes that robbed small amounts from different accounts. The strict standards for accounting that the chief auditor had set for the corporation always identified the leakage, and the miscreant was always dealt with harshly. The chief auditor relied on the head accountant at each location to enforce these standards, and in this case, McLeod was actually being a bit of a hindrance. A quick look at the numbers in question pointed to upwards of ten thousand dollars, and that was a personal slap in the face to the chief auditor.

He had requested a meeting with the president and laid out the problem in the Mexico operation. The president's instructions had been simple and direct, as always. "I want you to go to Mexico as soon as possible and correct these irregularities. Will this, in any way, affect the bottom line for the report to the board?"

"No. I can take care of that."

"See that you do exactly that. And one more thing. I have reviewed the numbers from Colorado, and as you know, the recent strikes have caused a drop in production at that location. I want you to prop these numbers up with production figures from Africa, and I want them set out in a way that your report to the board reflects the overall rise in numbers that we are truly experiencing."

It was always my report, he thought, when figures required shuffling. He preferred the word "reallocation."

"Yes, sir, that will be no problem."

"See that it's not. I want that report tomorrow, and then I want you to leave for Mexico."

The chief auditor had worked through the night and, after shaving and freshening up with a clean shirt from a stack he kept in his office, had personally handed the report to the president and then spent the rest of the day arranging for coverage during his absence.

The waiter brought the chief auditor's Beef Wellington to the table and removed the platter cover with a flourish. The chief auditor tested the crust with his fork and was pleased with the crispness of the lightly browned shell. As the waiter poured more wine, the auditor carefully and very precisely cut into the Wellington to preserve the appearance of the remaining crust so his last bite of the dish would look the same as the first.

Because he was a fussy man, he hated Mexico. He had been there once before, when they had opened their office in Sonora. He had found the people to be unsophisticated and out of touch with the world he knew and, more importantly, he despised the food. Mostly though, he hated the helter-skelter manner in which life was lived down there. There was a disregard for timelines, and although there was no real resistance to planning, they just could not follow the clear-cut paths of any plan. They lived no more than a day or two at a time down there. No, he was not going to enjoy this trip at all.

The headwaiter removed the plate, and his assistant brought a dish of Baked Alaska and set it in front of the chief auditor. The chief auditor's spirits rose. As the waiter poured his coffee, he felt the pure sensual pleasure of cutting into the dessert with a sterling silver spoon.

FIVE

J ones met Captain Wheeler and a tall, slender young man at the one-room storefront that served as the Ranger office in Tucson.

"Owen, this is John Trevor Ashley, our new recruit. Ashley, meet Owen Jones. Owen enlisted under Captain Rynning and has been with us for what, four years?"

"It'll be four years in November," Jones answered. He shook hands with the young man and turned back to the captain to hand him a piece of paper. "That's a signed confession from Pete Petersen that might shed some light on the MacDuff case." He and Ashley stood silent as the captain read the confession.

"A bad business!" The captain shook his head. "I'll need to talk more about this with you when we get back to headquarters. I'll get word to all the outposts to be on the lookout for the two ranch hands Pete talked about. As for the others, they're probably still in Mexico with Mitchell. This fellow Spence fits the description of someone who is wanted by the Pinkertons for a fraudulent stock scheme back East. It involved counterfeit stock certificates. The Pinks told me they thought he was headed for New Mexico or Arizona Territory. But counterfeiting and cattle rustling are worlds apart, and then throw in Mitchell and that bunch? Doesn't make sense."

"Unless he is a man of many talents." Ashley spoke up.

Jones and the captain looked at the new recruit in a way that clearly told him he had a lot to learn about law breakers.

"One thing is for sure, Owen. We need to find this Spence if he's the same guy that was with Mitchell and his bunch," the captain said. "Knowing Mitchell, I wonder if this Spence is still alive. Mitchell's never partnered up with anyone. That is, anyone that lived very long. I'll wire Colonel Kosterlitsky in Sonora. Maybe he'll have something we can use. In the meantime, I need you to hook up with the sheriff over in Greenlee County. He's got a rustling problem on his hands and asked for our help. He'll meet you at the train in Willcox. He's got a small posse, mounts, and pack animals waiting for you and Ashley."

Jones looked at the captain and shook his head. "I was certain we had run off most of the rustlers over there."

"This must be a new gang from New Mexico or Texas. Anyway, get on over there and bring this bunch in. I'm going back to Naco. You can reach me there."

The older ranger and the new recruit stepped out of the office and into the heat of downtown Tucson.

"John, I've got a chore to do over at the Palace Saloon, and if the captain hasn't assigned you another task, I need you as a witness."

"He said I was assigned to you until we get back to Naco. And by the way, my family calls me J.T." Ashley grinned.

They turned left onto Congress Street and walked over to the Palace Saloon. Jones asked for Janie Shaw. The bartender directed them to a boarding house on Second Street across the railroad tracks.

Several women lounged in the shade of the covered front porch of the boarding house and watched the rangers come up the front walk. They looked at the younger one with some interest but watched the older, hard-looking lawman's approach with suspicion. They were surprised when he doffed his hat and spoke to them as if they were fine ladies at a church social. He identified himself and his partner as Arizona Rangers and asked after Janie Shaw and her child, telling them he had a message for Janie. The oldest of the women met the rangers at the top of the steps and had been prepared to give them a hard time after watching them come up the walk, but she fought hard to maintain her distrust as the older man spoke to her softly and respectfully. She sent one of the younger women into the house to find Janie, and then she invited the rangers in for a drink. Jones apologized politely, saying they had to catch a train and just had time to do this favor for Janie's friend before they had to leave. The older woman and Jones were in the middle of a pleasant exchange about the weather when a plump blond with defeated eyes stepped out onto the porch.

"Miss Shaw?" Jones took off his hat.

"Yes?" Janie's eyes moved back and forth between the rangers.

"I have a message for you from Samuel Petersen."

"Who?" she asked.

"You might know him as Precious Pete."

"Oh, him! What does that no-good sonofabitch want?" Janie stared openly at Ashley.

"He asked me to bring something to you and his daughter, Sara."

"Sara?" She took her eyes off Ashley and looked at Jones. "Sara's not his daughter! I told him that a hunnert times."

The other girls on the porch put their hands to their mouths, trying to cover their giggles.

"He asked me to give Sara this." He handed Janie the gold piece and the ring.

"That sonofabitch! I knew it was him stole my ring. This was give to me by a fine gentleman, and I ain't seen it since the last time I seen Precious Pete."

There was a moment of silence, and the ranger let it go on a bit before asking in a soft voice, "And Sara?"

Janie turned to one of the younger girls. "Bonita, would you go fetch Sara? Pete always claimed Sara was his, but she ain't, and that's the truth of it." She held tightly to the ring and gold coin. Bonita came out onto the porch holding a small, towheaded little girl. The child looked at the rangers and then shyly buried her face in Bonita's shoulder. Just before the girl turned her head, Jones noticed crossed blue eyes and a large growth under her right ear.

"Well, I'm sure Pete wanted her to have it, just the same, and I promised him I'd bring it." The ranger put on his hat and turned to the older woman.

"Ma'am? May I have a word?" He nodded toward the front walk.

"My name is Anabelle Meeks. Miss Anabelle Meeks." She smiled at him and stepped down off the porch.

"Owen Jones, ma'am, pleased to make your acquaintance."

They strolled to the front of the property, turned left, and walked slowly to the end of the block. Jones briefly explained the circumstances of the MacDuff murders and described the men he was looking for. Miss Meeks had heard of Mitchell, but only by reputation. She did, however, know Ezekiel Bent. "A more evil man I have yet to meet!" She stopped and turned to the ranger. "He cut up a girl in Santa Fe. She lived, but after he was through with her face, she could never work again. She killed herself in El Paso, and I know that if Ezekiel Bent knew what she did, he would laugh his damn head off! I don't know the other names you mentioned, but I'll keep my ears open."

"I would appreciate it," Jones said. They began walking back to the house.

"How can I reach you if I hear anything about Bent or the rest?"

"You can always leave word for me at Ranger headquarters in Naco."

As they strolled up the walk, they heard Ashley laughing with the girls on the front porch.

"It seems like your handsome young partner is a big hit with the girls. I'd best get back before they start giving out free samples!"

Jones grinned and held Miss Meeks' elbow as she climbed the steps onto the porch.

"Ladies, it's been a genuine pleasure." He reached out and gently took the madam's hand, smiled at her, and then turned and walked down the steps to the sidewalk.

Janie got up from her chair and called after the rangers, "Where is Pete? Not that I give a damn, mind you!"

Jones stopped and looked back at Janie. "He's in Yuma prison."

"How long they keepin' him?" Janie had placed the ring on her finger and was fondling the gold piece.

"Not long. They're going to hang him for killing two ranch hands."

The madam smiled tightly and, liking the ranger's style, watched him and the younger one walk down the street in the direction of the train station.

"Learn anything from the girls?" Jones asked Ashley.

"Only that Janie truly did not like Pete. She told me all about the fancy gentleman that gave her that ring and about how Pete stole it from her. She showed me the ring, and I could see that the stone wasn't real. In fact, the whole thing was pretty cheap!"

"Well, that's pretty much the story of Pete and Janie's relationship. Don't you think, J.T.?"

"That's pretty philosophical." Ashley smiled.

"It may be, and I'm no philosopher, but knowing Pete like I do, I find it interesting that he believed in something ... hell, anything!"

"Even if it wasn't true?" Ashley asked.

"Men like Pete make things true in their own mind because it makes them feel better about so many failures in their pitiful little lives. Otherwise, I guess they may be forced to have to face up to who they really are." Jones changed the subject when he realized that it was starting to sound like a lecture. "And that young'un he claimed was his? Well, she sure as hell is starting life with the deck stacked against her." Jones shook his head.

"Speaking of stacked decks, did you learn anything from the madam?"

Jones stopped and looked at Ashley. "Miss Anabelle Meeks knows one of the killers by the name of Ezekiel Bent. Said he was a real bad one. I asked her to call me at headquarters if she hears anything. I might have learned more, but I was anxious to get back since I was concerned that a certain gallant young ranger might catch something soap and water wouldn't wash off."

Ashley's face turned red, and he looked straight ahead.

He could not be sure if Jones was joking with him.

They crossed over the railroad tracks and walked toward downtown.

"You hungry, J.T.?"

"I'm nearly always hungry." Ashley gave a relieved grin.

"We have a couple of hours before the train leaves, and it is Ranger tradition to buy the new recruit's first meal, so let's get us a steak at the Alameda. Probably be the last decent meal we'll have for a spell. It's going to be a while until we get to Greenlee County."

"Have you bought many recruits their first meal?" Ashley asked him.

"Nope." Jones turned off Alameda onto Sixth Avenue. "You're the first."

Ashley noticed a spring in Jones's step. The older ranger suddenly seemed to be in fine spirits. Had he known Jones better, he would know that the man was indeed in fine spirits, as he always was when he thought of leaving town for a long scout in the open spaces of Arizona Territory.

SIX

H e took two blows from his opponent, an older boy who outweighed him by twenty pounds. The first, a left jab, caught him above his right eye. The second, a straight right that his opponent telegraphed, glanced off his left ear as he ducked his head. The larger boy was dancing, confident and light on his feet. Owen was patient, waiting for an opening, and when his opponent dropped his left hand while circling to his right, Owen shot a powerful right to his opponent's cheek that stung the knuckles of his closed fist and stunned the other boy, who dropped both hands while trying to gain his balance. It was then that the small, skinny Owen delivered a left-right combination over his opponent's lowered hands. His fists slashed as if they had a will of their own. He moved quickly, viciously closing the gap, and as the larger boy fell back, Owen smashed another combination into the boy's face. Blood flew, and the older boy's eyes began to swell up. Still Owen's fists struck as the older boy, completely stunned now and with no control of his legs, fell into the ropes. Owen set his weight squarely over his feet and threw solid punches into the boy's body, left, right, left, right, and the larger boy sagged against the ropes and then fell to the canvas floor of the ring.

"That's enough, Owen!" Father O'Casey yelled as he stepped between the two pugilists. The priest's bulk and whiskey breath broke Owen's focus on his opponent. He backed away and looked at the other boy. It was hard to tell that his opponent was taller and heavier as he lay flat on his back, blood bubbling out of his nose and mouth, his face a wreck. Owen studied him a moment and then walked slowly back to his corner of the ring to sit on the stool.

Owen had been fighting other boys in the home as far back as his memory would reach. His first memories of anything were of his life in the home. When Father O'Casey had arrived at the home, he had organized a boxing club and taught the boys the fine art of pugilism as a way of controlling their fighting. At first Owen had not trusted him, but he had eventually found Father O'Casey to be different from the other priests. Father O'Casey always spoke quietly as if he were speaking through the screen of the confessional. His battered face and cauliflower ears made Owen wonder if the priest had ever won a fight in his life, but there was a peacefulness, like a quiet cloud, surrounding the priest, and as time passed, Owen had learned to trust him and value his observations.

"Your fists are even faster than your temper, m' lad. You must learn to control that temper and let your fists do what they will. If you can do that, you'll have more than an even chance of holding your own," the priest told him one Sunday after Mass.

Owen left the home two weeks before his fourteenth birthday. He was apprenticed to a ship's chandler on the riverfront but abandoned the apprenticeship after a year and worked odd jobs on the docks. When he heard about Father O' Casey's illness, he went back to the home but was told that the priest was at Charity Hospital.

Owen walked past the beds in the hospital ward to the end of the room where the nun had pointed out Father O'Casey's bed. The priest looked old and gray, and Owen knew that he was near the end. The

*dull film left the old man's eyes when he saw the boy, and he grabbed
Owen's hand in a strong grip.*

"It's glad I am that you came, lad." He smiled a tired smile.

*"How are you, Father?" He felt foolish as soon as the question left
his lips.*

*"I'm waiting for my appointment with St. Peter, but, alas, he must
be busy, for he's kept me waitin' a good while now. And you, lad, how
are you?" The father studied Owen's face closely and saw the twice-
broken nose and the tissue beginning to thicken around his eyes.
"Don't tell me, Owen! You're still fightin'?!"*

"Just on Sundays, Father."

"For money, then?"

"Yes, Father. Prize fights on the docks."

"Have you made much?"

"I have a few hundred set aside."

*"Listen to me, then. I speak to you not as a priest but as an old
fighter. Take the money and leave. Get out of this place. Go west,
California maybe. There's no future for ya here, and sure there's no
future in fightin' for money. You're here for a reason, lad, and I'll
wager that it's not fightin' for money. Go, for God's sake, and find the
reason. There's a lot of good in ya, lad, and you've got a lot of good to
give. So go find the reason He put you here. Promise an old dyin'
priest that!" He sank back on his pillow, exhausted.*

"I promise, Father."

*"And one more thing, Owen. You're a good fighter, but not great.
You have a God-given quickness, but I could never teach you to move
and punch. You always bore straight in. A good fighter will see that
and destroy you. So give up this fightin' for money!"*

*Father O'Casey's eyes closed, and Owen sat watching him sleep and
thought about what he had said. After a while, Owen got up and left
the hospital. He stopped at the cathedral to light a candle and say a
prayer for the old priest, but he felt like a hypocrite. He remained*

kneeling in the pew, staring straight ahead without seeing the altar. He was thinking about Father O'Casey and his own life at the home. He tried again to pray, but he felt empty. The light streamed through the stained-glass windows of the cathedral, making bright patterns on the steps of the altar. He remembered the comfort and safety he had always felt as a young boy at the altar when he had served Mass. And then he felt the sadness that always came to him as young boy just before he cried, and he remembered the first and only time Father O'Casey had caught him crying. The priest had spoken to him gently but firmly.

"So what are you going to do, lad? Sit there crying like a little girl, or will you go about solving your problem?"

SEVEN

Sheriff Swenson and his deputy met the rangers at the train in Willcox. As they rode north to Solomonville, he filled them in on the details of his cattle-rustling problem. Rustlers had been stealing livestock and horses from ranches large and small throughout eastern Arizona. They were even stealing horses from the Apache reservation. Some of the stolen cattle had been found by livestock inspectors as far west as Globe and as far east as Lordsburg, New Mexico Territory. Swenson had been working with other lawmen in Arizona and New Mexico, and they all were convinced that the rustlers had a base in the mountains of New Mexico, which allowed them to move freely back and forth between the two territories. The ranchers had put together five hundred dollars in reward money, which created a lot of interest in the rustlers' capture. Jones listened and asked questions, keeping his skepticism to himself. Rewards had a way of introducing characters onto the scene who were every bit as unsavory as the criminals, and Jones had little faith in these reward seekers.

He asked about the other members of the posse who were waiting in Solomonville and was told that they were a deputy, two small ranchers who had lost cattle to the thieves, and two Apaches from the White River Reservation who were looking for the stolen Indian ponies. Swenson vouched for the ranchers as solid citizens, and he said he had worked with the Indians in the past and trusted them. The younger of the two Indians was a reservation police officer who had been educated back East, and the older one had been a scout for General Crook in the eighties. The sheriff agreed with Jones that the best plan would be a wide-ranging scout to the north, as far as the Black River, covering all the east-west routes.

They rode into Solomonville at dusk. The sheriff set the rangers up in a small shack behind his stables. The Indians were camped north of the rangers, close to the river. Jones set about checking their mounts, equipment, and weapons, and then he and Ashley inventoried their supplies and made a list of items to purchase at the general store. After finishing these chores, they went into the shack. Jones had just lit the lamp in the small room when the sheriff hurried in.

"Bad news, I'm afraid. A foreman who works on a spread about forty miles west came in late this afternoon while we were riding up here and reported about sixty head of cattle stolen." Sheriff Swenson had a worried look on his face.

"He knows for certain they're stolen and not just missing?" Ashley surprised Jones with his question. The sheriff looked at Ashley, annoyed at this impertinence.

"He's fairly certain, Ranger. Two of his best hands were found shot dead, their guns and horses gone, too. I reckon we can call that a damn clue, don't you?"

Ashley looked down, embarrassed.

"It happened yesterday. The rancher and some of his men started tracking the herd north toward the Gilas, but the foreman doesn't know how long they'll stay on the trail." The sheriff had turned back to the older ranger.

Ashley stood quietly in the corner, his embarrassment turning to sullenness. Jones called him over and quietly asked him to go get the Indians and then arrange for the supplies at the general store. He turned back to Swenson. "Give me the details about the cattle—their brand, breed, and such—and I'll get started tonight, head north and try to cut their trail before they either get rid of the livestock or get too far ahead of us."

The sheriff nodded. "I gotta get over to the ranch and handle my coroner duties, so you'll have to make do without me. I'll send my deputy and the two ranchers over right now. The deputy will have all the details you need."

After the sheriff left, Jones walked out and put more wood on the fire before filling a coffeepot full of water, dumping in two handfuls of ground coffee, and putting it on the makeshift grill over the fire. He was thinking about the dead cowboys and tried to smother the feeling that the bad news of their death was a good thing for him. His quarry now faced a hanging, and he had a fresh trail to find. It just made the whole situation a lot simpler.

Jones stood at the fire and studied his posse. He remembered the young Indian policeman, Antonio from a rustling case he had worked north of Safford. The young man was smart and dedicated, and had been a big help in solving the case. The older Indian sat quiet and still, ignoring the others around the fire. The corners of his mouth were pulled down in a permanent scowl. He reminded Jones of a photograph of Geronimo he had seen in the newspaper. The ranchers, Bob and Lloyd, had been in the territory most of their lives and were friendly and easygoing. It was plain that they would be comfortable on a long ride. The young deputy named Billy wore a new Stetson without a smudge or sweat stain. He appeared to be a bit of a dude and fidgeted nervously. Jones would keep an eye on him. He briefed the men on the rustling and murder of the two cowboys and of his plans to leave that night and head north.

Jones laid out his plans for the first leg of their scout and then inspected the weapons and ammunition. One of the ranchers had a Spanish Mauser, the older Indian carried a '79 Springfield, and the others, like the rangers, had '95 Winchester .30-40 rifles. All carried sidearms. He told them to get a good meal and meet at the shack in three hours.

Jones banked down the fire and then went into the shack and sat on the floor, placing a small square of canvas in front of him. He put his Winchester and Colt on the cloth and began cleaning the weapons. He began by carefully wiping the mixture of old oil and dust from the moving parts and then used a small brush to clean areas he could not reach with the rag. He was meticulous about the care of his weapons and even went so far as to remove the cartridges from his belt and wipe them down with a rag. The ritual of cleaning the guns always filled him with a sense of ease and contentment that came with a simple task that did not require a lot of thought. Ashley came in with a box of supplies and put it in the corner. He began taking cans and sacks out of the box, carefully separating them by size and shape so he could repack them on the mule. He worked methodically without saying a word.

"That was a fair question you asked the sheriff." Jones was replacing the cylinder of the Colt. Ashley grunted, left the room, and returned in a moment with several large squares of canvas.

"Sit down a minute and listen to me," the older ranger instructed.

Ashley sat on the cot, his face still showing signs of humiliation.

"If we're going to ride together, I need to know if you're going to let your pride get in the way of our mission. I need to know about any questions or ideas you might have, and the only way that can happen is if we talk. But most of all, I need to know if you're the type that clouds up every time your feelings get hurt."

"No! I'm not like that." Ashley looked down at the floor.

"Look, J.T., rangers are asked to go against outlaws in places the sheriffs can't or won't go. We are almost always outnumbered and outgunned, but that's the game we chose. So if we are asked to do these things, then we have a perfect right to ask all the damn questions we want, because mostly, all we have going for us is information. We have to know as much as possible about the crime, the outlaws, the lawmen, the terrain, and everything else. And the best way to get this information is by asking. So never, ever pass up the opportunity to talk with folks, and then listen real carefully to what they have to say. Understand?"

"I understand."

"What did you hear when the sheriff answered your question?"

"I got the feeling he didn't like being questioned."

"Why do you think that is?"

"Pride?"

"Could be. It also could be he's a mite nervous about not being able to solve this rustling problem in his territory and he's probably catching a lot of hell from the ranchers and other citizens that elected him. Could be other reasons, too, but the fact is we learned a little about the sheriff and his operation just 'cause you asked the question." Jones handed his cleaning kit to the younger ranger. "I'll open a can of beans and some hash while you clean your weapons. Do you have the receipt from the store?" Ashley handed him the receipt, and Jones folded it carefully and put it in the oilskin pouch.

The seven-man posse left Solomonville before eleven o'clock, heading north under a half moon. Jones reckoned they would break the rustlers' trail shortly after dawn. The chill of the night air staved off his drowsiness, and the freedom of ranging in open country under a clear night sky lifted his spirits. The sound of leather creaking and hooves breaking the crust of the desert ground came to him through the sharp, crisp air, and he couldn't think of anyplace he would rather be. He rode out front with the old scout on his right.

They stopped for a quick cold breakfast just after first light and then continued on over the flats north of the Gilas. Jones had taken the center and spread the rest of the posse out with about one hundred yards between them. Just after noon, the rancher on the far left flank signaled that he had found the tracks they were looking for. The herd was moving to the northeast, and Chapo, the old scout, estimated there to be about forty head of cattle. He pointed out tracks of two outriders, one on each side of the herd.

"I figure they'll have one or two at point and another one or two ridin' drag," the older rancher said. "And Bob and I figure we know where they're headed. There's some good meadows and water east in the mountains. It's a little late in the season but still decent grazin'."

"Las Vegas del Oso," Antonio said.

"Yep. Bear Meadows," Lloyd, one of the ranchers, agreed. "If they were moving direct to there from the ranch they should be damn close by now. My cousin got a spread about ten miles east of here. It won't take us out of our way, and Bob and I reckon we can leave the pack animals there, get some fresh water, and move up to the meadows a mite quicker."

Jones nodded. He was thinking.

"If we leave now, we could get close to the meadows before midnight." The rancher named Bob looked to the ranger for a decision.

Jones considered his options. If they rode until dark, they would have closed a considerable distance and be far enough away from the gang to build a fire, eat a decent meal, get some sleep, and then jump the gang about midday. But if there was delay of any sort, they would be wasting daylight hours. Besides, he thought, the gang would spread out with the herd after breakfast and make it more difficult for the posse to control the situation, and he did not like the idea of losing the element of surprise. He planned to get the rustlers and cattle down off the mountain as quickly as possible, and he needed all the daylight he could get to do it right.

His other choice was to make an approach at night. They would still have the light of the half moon and could fix the gang's location before moving into position to be ready for action at first light. He decided on this plan of action, and when he told the men, old Chapo nodded and looked at the ranger with a touch less hostility.

They rode east to the cousin's ranch, and while they took ammunition and light supplies from the pack animals, the rancher's wife made coffee and fried up a slab of bacon to go with the biscuits left over from breakfast.

They pushed hard during the remaining daylight and stopped at a small stream just inside the foothills an hour before sunset to rest and water the horses. The ranchers and the Indians were familiar with the meadows and described the terrain to the rangers. There were actually two meadows separated by a low, rocky hill that ran north and south. At the south boundary of the meadows was a small stream that flowed west to east. This was where the rustlers would probably set up camp. The cattle would most likely be in a small depression next to the stream. This area was like a natural corral that could hold a hundred head so one cowboy could easily watch the whole herd.

They left their resting spot and after an hour of a gentle but steady climb, they were within a half mile of the approach to the meadows. They moved their horses into the scrub cedar at the base of the mountain. Jones instructed the men to get some rest and told Ashley to make sure no one built a fire. Jones wanted to scout the meadow from the top of the large hill overlooking the outlaws' camp. He asked Antonio if he and his uncle would go with him since they knew the area well. They agreed and with the Indians leading, Jones rode to the bottom of the large hill. The three left their horses hobbled at the foot of this hill that formed the southern rim of the meadows and began climbing to the top. Jones climbed carefully, picking his way up the slope in the moonlight. The air was crisp and thin, and he felt his lungs struggle to bring in enough oxygen. The old scout took the lead, and Jones envied his effortless pace. The man moved easily, as if he were moving over flat land. The younger Indian moved parallel with the older one, out on his right about fifty feet. The scout would look back at Jones from time to time, challenging him with his eyes. Jones paid him no mind. He was thinking of his posse and how he meant to use them in the morning.

Soon they came to a fast-running stream. The Indians stopped and scooped water into their mouths. Jones stopped and sat on a rock to catch his breath. His legs were unsteady and he was lightheaded.

He watched the water curl in sparkling ribbons over the dark, slick rocks and straighten into uneven lengths as it ran over the bottom pebbles before rising and curling again on the large rocks below. It looked like a bow coming undone in the rain. The younger Indian moved back out to the flank, and the scout squatted beside the stream, his eyes on the ranger.

Jones felt the calm of the mountainside under the half-moon with no sound except his ragged breathing and the water gurgling over the rocks. He put his hand in the stream and was shocked by the cold. He sipped some water and then left his hand in the stream. His fingers quickly became numb from the snowmelt as he followed the water's flow with his eyes and watched it tumble out of sight between two boulders fifty feet down the mountain. He wondered how far downstream the water would have to run before it was no longer cold enough to numb him. He looked up and saw the old scout sign that they could see the meadows just ahead of where the younger Indian stood looking back at them. Jones got up and started the climb to the top.

From the top they looked out over the meadow. The best approach, he thought, would be from the trees north of the meadow, where they could stage before making their final approach across the grass. He could see a low grass-covered ridge running east and west, about halfway across the meadow. From his position he could not determine how high it was, but it might offer some concealment after they moved out from the tree line. The gang had few options for escape. They could ride west along the stream but would eventually have to turn north to get to the mouth of the valley. Jones could easily shift to his right to cut that escape route. To the south was the mountain, which was a steep, long climb in the open and would have to be made on foot.

To the east along the stream was the only possibility of escape. The stream ran between the slope of the mountain and the rocky hill to the east. There was room to get through there on horseback. Jones would have to cover that. He lay there a while longer, committing the terrain to memory and making plans for his approach in the morning. Then he looked at the Indians and motioned with his head. They began their climb down the mountain.

When they got back to the others, Jones briefed them on the terrain and their assignments. Ashley and Antonio would cover the eastern end of the stream. When they had a chance, they were to check the brands on the cattle and get an accurate count. Jones, Chapo, and the deputy would be the left flank on the approach. The ranchers would be on their right. If any of the gang tried to run to the west, the ranchers would turn right and cut off their escape. Jones would cover the main body at the camp. They were to go in quick and quiet, and Jones would be the only one to talk to the rustlers. There was to be no shooting without his command, but if the rustlers started anything, the posse was free to fire at will.

They checked their weapons one more time and then quietly and slowly moved into the canyon and into the trees on the northern edge of the meadow. Jones knew they needed to rest as much as possible before first light. They slept with one man on watch in one-hour shifts. Jones took the first watch and sat near the edge of the trees to watch the reflected light of the rustlers' fire over the grassy mound in the middle of the meadow, and was satisfied that it was high enough to mask their approach. The temperature had dropped, and he felt the chill in his bones. Like almost everyone in the Ranger Company, he preferred the heat of the desert to the cold of the mountains. He wrapped a blanket closer around his shoulders and massaged a cramp in his right hand. He cut a fresh piece of tobacco from a plug and put it in his mouth but took it out after a while when it did not produce its usual stimulating effect. So he sat there numb, fighting sleep and watching the firelight dance against the shadow of the south hills of the meadow, and he thought about far-off west Texas.

They had left Fort Stockton and were on the trail to Fort Davis. Sergeant Sutton came up next to Jones and rode alongside in silence for a while. The sergeant was an ornery old veteran and did not speak with the younger rangers except to give orders or discuss plans of the day, so Jones was surprised that he would even ride alongside in silence.

"I have fought Indians for what seems like my whole life, and I learned you can never trust them or give them an even break. And you can never expect them to think like a white man, 'cause they can't—they don't have it in 'em. You can't know what they'll do next, 'cause mostly, they don't know what they'll do next. But you can watch 'em and study them, and pretty soon, you'll start to understand them a little. When you do that, then you can beat 'em. That's how we beat the Comanche."

Jones was so surprised by the sergeant's discourse, he did not respond.

Sergeant Sutton went on. "Rangers studied them, began thinking like them, and then started fightin' like them. When the Comanches raided, they killed every man, woman, and child they didn't take with them for slaves, and they burned ranches and killed what cattle they didn't steal. We learned to ride harder and faster than them and kill every one of them we come across. And we burnt their tepees and killed all their animals. We snuck up on them, laid ambushes, and blew the shit out of them before they knew we were there. They never did learn to think like us, but we sure as hell learned to think like them. And that was the beginning of the end for them. They skedaddled every time they knew we were around."

Jones remembered being full of pride that the sergeant would talk to him about the times of the Comanche. He had heard younger rangers ask the sergeant about fighting Indians, but the old veteran would just shrug and say he was not a storyteller and warn them that they had best be more interested in handling their chores than hearing old war stories.

They rode alongside each other in silence while Jones tried to form an intelligent question to ask the sergeant.

"Funny thing," the sergeant began again, "when we took and turned their ways against 'em, well, that's probably the only time they feared us. And now they're gone!" He said it as if he found it hard to

believe. He was quiet for a while. "By God! I never felt so ready to start the day as I did when we was set against the Comansh!"

Jones found his voice. "It sounds like you miss 'em, Sergeant."

Sergeant Sutton turned slowly in the saddle and fixed Jones with a look so scornful that he remembered it to this day. It was the look the sergeant gave younger rangers when he felt they were wasting his time. The sergeant looked at the flustered young ranger a bit longer and then rode off without saying another word.

Jones was losing his fight with sleep now. The warmth of the blanket and the dancing firelight across the meadow fought against him and won, and he fell into a dead sleep. He did not sleep long and woke with a start to find Ashley sitting against a tree next to him, his eyes fixed in the direction of the rustlers' camp.

"I couldn't sleep," Ashley said. He gave no indication that Jones had been asleep. "It won't be long 'til first light. Why don't you close your eyes a while, and I'll wake you when it's time." Ashley kept his eyes fixed straight ahead as he spoke.

Jones fell asleep instantly, without a word, and after what seemed a very short time, Ashley shook his shoulder.

"It's time to go," he said and went to alert the others. They readied their horses quietly in the early light, and Jones was surprised to see the old scout dressed in an enlisted man's blue fatigue blouse and wearing a bright red headband. There was a shiny medal pinned to the left breast of the blouse.

As planned, Ashley and Antonio led their horses east through the trees to the rocky hills. When Jones saw them come out of the trees and move in the direction of the stream, he motioned the others forward. They walked their horses to the crown in the meadow and then mounted and rode toward the camp.

One of the rustlers was bringing wood to the fire, and when he looked up and saw the posse at the edge of their camp, he stood speechless, staring at them as if they were ghosts riding through the dew of the meadow.

"Good morning!" Jones called out.

Jones and his men carried their rifles at the ready. The rustler stood there with his arms full of wood, knowing something was not quite right but unable to move.

"We are Arizona Rangers, and we mean to check the brands on that herd of cattle!" Jones announced. The morning light revealed three other men at the edge of the camp.

Another rustler moved closer to the fire and spoke to Owen. "You are welcome to it, Cap'n. Get down and have some coffee. Y'all must be cold from ridin' all night." He looked closely at the deputy. "That you, Billy?" he asked the young man.

"Yep, it's me. How you doin', Tim?"

"Fine, fine. Get down and have some breakfast. We got a lot of catchin' up to do!" The rustler smiled good-naturedly. "Wait!" Jones motioned to the deputy to stop, but he had already dismounted and was walking toward the fire and was now between the mounted men and the rustlers.

"We heard you become a lawman, Billy." Tim laughed. As Billy walked forward to shake hands, Tim drew his pistol in a smooth motion and shot the deputy in the face. The other rustlers, caught unawares, began grabbing for their pistols and rifles. Jones marked their locations in his mind and brought his rifle to his shoulder. Tim calmly stood his ground, took aim, and began firing at the mounted men. Jones moved smoothly but quickly, firing three times. The reports of the three rounds from his rifle were so closely spaced that their echoes off the mountain sounded like one loud boom. The first round hit the one called Tim in the chest, the second dropped a rustler who was standing on the other side of the fire, holding a rifle, and the last struck a rustler aiming a pistol at him. He had already fixed those targets during his approach and was now looking for others when he heard a Colt crack at the edge of the trees. As he swung in that direction, the boom of Chapo's old Springfield almost deafened him, and he saw another rustler go down. The smell of the black powder from the Springfield was sharp in the absolute silence that followed the fight. Jones motioned the others to dismount, and they watched him as he slid out of the saddle and kept his horse between him and the camp, his rifle aimed over the saddle. They heard another crack from the Colt in the trees, followed by the crack of a Winchester. He hollered for Ashley.

"J.T.! You OK?"

"We're OK! Got one wounded here. We'll bring him in!" Ashley replied.

"Move up the creek toward us and holler out when you get to the trees!" Jones ordered.

"OK!"

Jones moved carefully, staying at the side of his horse as he moved closer to the fallen rustlers. He walked by Billy the dude deputy, who appeared to be dead, a hole above his left eye. The rustler called Tim was moaning and holding his chest. The ranger picked up Tim's pistol and told the ranchers to carefully check the condition of the other rustlers and then squatted down next to the wounded rustler.

"Goddamit! You done killed me!" Tim spat at the ranger.

"Well now, Tim, we don't know how bad it is. Besides, you done for the deputy and was trying for the rest of us." Jones spoke quietly. "Let me have a look."

He unbuttoned Tim's shirt and saw the hole just to the left of center of his chest. Must have missed the heart and main artery, he thought when he didn't see a lot of blood, but no doubt the bullet went through a lung.

"Well, Tim, it doesn't look that bad. Appears you may be lucky," Jones lied in a calm voice.

"You lyin' old bastard!" There was no hope in Tim's eyes.

"Why were you so quick to shoot Billy?" Jones asked him in a conversational tone.

"That son of a bitch is shirttail kin on my mama's side, and we heard he was lookin' to turn us in for a reward!" Tim still had some spirit, and there was anger and betrayal in his voice.

"That may be, but he was a lawman and that's a hangin' offense. So whether you die up here or on the gallows, it looks like your time is short. You have a chance to square things and tell me about the rustling and who's buying the cattle and—"

"You can go to hell, you old bastard—" Tim grimaced and broke off in a groan. Pink foam was blowing out of his mouth as he tried to suck in air.

It won't be long now, Jones thought. Definitely lung shot.

"Tim, I'd like to know if you ever done business with a man named Spence or a half-breed named Mitchell?"

Tim groaned and stared back, hatred in his eyes. But the hatred, along with the light in his eyes, was fading. Jones knew he would get no more out of this one.

"We're in the trees!" Ashley hollered. "OK! Come on in!" Jones called.

Owen went over to look at the other rustlers, and he thought of the sheriff and how he had not mentioned the deputy's connection to the rustlers. The outlaw who Chapo had shot was almost bled out, the Springfield's big round having gone through his arm, his ribcage, and out the other side just about dead center. Probably hit the big artery. Jones was impressed with the old Indian's marksmanship. The two other men Jones had shot were dead. He noticed that the bullet holes were lower in the center of their bodies than he expected. He frowned and could have sworn that he had been holding higher than that. He walked over to the fire and poured a cup of the rustlers' coffee.

Ashley and the young Indian carried a wounded man over and laid him down next to the fire. Jones was struck by the youth of the wounded rustler. He looked to be a teenager. He was shot high in the chest, just under his left shoulder, and Jones hoped it wasn't fatal. He needed answers to some questions.

"Who shot him?' Jones asked Ashley.

"I did." Ashley was placing a rolled-up blanket under the wounded boy's head. Jones unbuttoned the boy's shirt.

"What's your name, son?"

"Ah—" The boy tried to speak, but his mouth was dry. His face was pale and his eyes reflected fear. He closed his mouth and slowly moved his tongue around, searching for moisture.

Jones held his cup to the young man's lips. "Here. Have some of this."

The young man sipped some coffee.

"Take your time, son. Looks like the bullet went clean through. You'll be fine." His voice was soothing, reassuring.

Tears filled the rustler's eyes. "I wasn't trying to shoot nobody!"

"I'm sure you weren't, son. Now don't worry; we're gonna patch you up and get you to a doctor. What's your name?"

"Johnny Richardson." Pain crept into the boy's face.

Well hallelujah, Jones thought, recognizing the one of the names Precious Pete had given him. "Johnny, we got some tincture of laudanum over there with some other stuff to patch you up and ease the pain, and we got a lot to talk about. You up to it?"

"I reckon, but I gotta know how much trouble I'm in." Jones could see that the boy trusted him and wanted to talk.

He poured a fresh cup of coffee and then began questioning the boy in a low, calm voice. He explained how he would testify on his behalf and assured the boy that he was not facing the hangman. Then slowly and meticulously, he began getting out of him everything that the young man knew about Spence, Mitchell, and the MacDuff murders. Within thirty minutes, the boy grew tired and was having trouble keeping his eyes open.

Jones noticed that his face was growing pale, and even though he needed more information, he stopped his questioning and let Ashley and Antonio dress the boy's wound. He left the young man and went over to the fire and sat with the posse. Chapo had found tracks of two shod horses leading west to the entrance of the canyon. Two other men who were with the gang had either gone for supplies or left for good; they could not tell, but it was unlikely that they would return any time soon. After settling on the number of cows and their brands and after signing a receipt, the ranchers agreed to take on the task of moving the cattle and the horses of the murdered cowboys off the mountain. The rangers would take the bodies of the deputy and the rustlers and the wounded young man to Clifton, and the Indians would return to the reservation with the recovered ponies.

When the ranchers went to tend to the cattle, Antonio asked the rangers to come over to the stream, where the older scout sat on a large flat rock. "My uncle wants to tell you something. He understands English but wants to speak through me in his own language."

Jones looked at the old scout. It was only then that he noticed a bloody hole in the sleeve of the army coat.

"Dammit! I didn't know he was hit!" He turned to Antonio.

"No!" The younger Indian was almost frantic. "I mean, please, he does not want to acknowledge that it is a matter of any consequence!" He looked pleadingly at Jones.

Jones backed off, impressed with the old man's stand and his nephew's command of the English language. The older man began speaking in his language, looking directly at the ranger.

"He says …" the young man began. "Let me explain something first. My uncle is old-fashioned. He rode with General Crook against the Chiricahuas and—" At the word "Chiricahua," the old man began speaking harshly to his nephew in his language. It was clear to the rangers that no matter the language, he was giving the young man hell. After the tirade, the young Indian turned to the rangers.

"He does not want me to tell you too much about him. His generation thinks it is a sign of weakness to talk about one's self. He wants me to tell you that he has not liked many white men, but he wants to hunt the bad man again with you. He said with the Indians on the reservation and the war with the whites and other Indians over, the bad man is the only man he can hunt and fight. He says he would track him and fight him with you any time."

Jones and the old man had been looking directly at each other during this exchange, and Jones had not detected any change in the Indian's facial expression, nor did his eyes give away any feelings.

"Tell your uncle," Jones said, continuing to look at the old man, "it was an honor to fight at the side of a warrior like him and I look forward to a time in the future when I can do it again."

The young man translated. When he was finished, the old man nodded seriously, and the only change Jones noted in his expression was a small bit of a sparkle that passed briefly over his dark eyes. The old man nodded again and walked back to the camp.

The young Indian watched him walk away. "He is old-fashioned, but he supported my going to college when the others in our clan did not. He respected General Crook more than any white man he ever knew, and when the general pinned that medal on him, my mother said it was the only time she saw him come close to smiling. He will go back to the reservation with his wound and he will be the envy of his peers. The wound is another medal to him because, to him and his generation, a life without fighting is no life at all."

The young policeman shook hands with Jones and Ashley and walked over to his waiting uncle. After wishing him well, the rangers stood by the little stream, watching him and his uncle lead their string of ponies over the meadow to the mouth of the canyon. Weariness covered Jones like a blanket; he wanted nothing more than to sit on one of the flat rocks and listen to the water roll by. The young boy Richardson had not furnished much information of value about Spence, Mitchell, or the others in the gang, and to add to Jones's disappointment, his bones ached, his piles were aggravating him, and he had a sore throat. *What was it the rustler, Tim, called me? An old bastard?* He chuckled to himself. *Maybe I really am starting to feel my age.*

"Hey, Ranger!" It was one of the ranchers over by the fire. "Your prisoner just died!"

Ashley turned and looked at Jones, a mixture of surprise and guilt on his face.

"You ever kill a man before?" he asked Ashley.

"No. It's—I mean—I never have!" Ashley looked lost.

"Come on, J.T. We got a lot to talk about on the way back." Jones no longer felt tired or old. He was just glad to be alive.

EIGHT

―――――◆―――――

Edgar McLeod, senior vice-president of accounting of the Consolidated Mineral and Mining Corporation at Cananea, Mexico, was sweating as he hurried across the plaza. The sweat ran over his scalp and down his neck to the boiled collar of his shirt, turning the crisp white edge to a soggy fold. He was sweating for two very good reasons. The first was that he knew he was weeks away, at best, from being discovered as the author of a scheme he had originally intended to be a short-term pilferage that he could easily hide in his ledgers. But the scheme had proven so lucrative that he had run it out and enlarged it well past the point of petty larceny, and now the chief auditor from New York was on his way to Cananea to personally conduct an on-site audit of the company's Sonora operation.

The second reason waited for him across the plaza at the Mar Pacifico Hotel. He was to meet an old colleague and kick off the beginning of an intricate scheme involving the mining company. McLeod's role was to deliver to this colleague inside information on stockholders and affiliated brokerage houses, as well as several authentic stock certificates. The problem was that he did not have this information, and because of the pending on-site audit, he would not be able to obtain it. He cursed as he felt the heat radiate off the flagstones of the plaza.

Spence sat in an overstuffed leather chair and looked across the white marble floor of the lobby through the front windows of the hotel. His mind was busy with dates, schedules, locations, and all the other logistical details of his plan. He had just turned to look at the large clock on the wall over the bell desk when he saw McLeod walk through the front doors. McLeod stood for a moment to enjoy the cool shade of the lobby, looked around, spotted Spence, and walked over to him.

Their relationship was not one that required much in the way of greetings and small talk, so after a quick handshake, they got down to particulars.

"Our friend is set up in the capital and can begin work as soon as I deliver the certificates," Spence said.

"There is a problem." McLeod's voice had a squeak to it.

Spence leaned back in his chair and sighed. "A problem?" He tried to look into McLeod's eyes, but McLeod was nervously looking around the room.

"I, that is …"

Spence noticed McLeod sweating in the cool of the lobby. "Go on," he said.

McLeod stammered through his explanation of how he had created fictional contractors and service companies and paid them in company funds for nonexistent goods and labor. He explained how he had been able to short-stop the bills and, because of the dollar threshold of his authority, direct company checks to accounts he had set up himself. He had started out charging the company small amounts, but when he had found that these figures were easily absorbed into the monthly expense sheets, he had expanded the scheme until the numbers had become so large that they were no longer invisible and a thorough audit would uncover the whole scheme. He then told Spence about the imminent arrival in Mexico of the chief auditor.

Spence sat still, absorbing the details of McLeod's story. He quickly explored the potential damage to his plans and then considered the profits McLeod had gained from his petty fraud on the company books. He was surprised at the idiocy of McLeod's actions. They had worked hard in setting up the counterfeit stock certificate scheme. He ran a quick inventory in his mind; the printer and equipment in Mexico City, the brokers in New York and Paris, the schedules for trips, meetings, and conferences and other elements of the complex scheme. He controlled a flash of anger and deliberately concentrated on trying to salvage the operation.

"How much time do we have?" he asked.

"Two, three weeks at the most. But time is not the problem."

"And what is the problem?" Spence tried to be patient.

"My access has been limited. It is company policy to temporarily suspend the accountant's duties when an internal audit is scheduled. I no longer have control of the books, invoicing, work orders, and all the rest. And I don't have access to the corporate documents, and that means I can't get the certificates. Normally this suspension would last only until the audit is complete, and then I would return to my normal duties."

"In short, you were pulling a false billing scheme. I can't believe you would screw up a million-dollar deal for a nickel-and-dime false billing grift. So when the audit finds your ghost companies and billing, it's all over for you. Is that it?'

"Yes. I'm afraid so." All the strength went out of McLeod, and he sank back into his chair, staring blankly past Spence.

Spence was quiet, exploring every possibility while McLeod continued to sweat in his overstuffed chair. He was left with no choice but to accept the fact that his plan for the counterfeit certificates was dead, yet he knew he could not dwell on frustration over the lost time, effort, and considerable investment he had laid out. Spence fought back the urge to reach across the table and choke the life out of this miserable excuse of a bookkeeper, and his mind began to work on salvaging something from McLeod's remaining time at the company.

"What job did they give you during the audit period?" Spence asked casually.

"I've been assigned to assist the payroll department. I don't have any real control over anything but will be assigned tasks from the department head."

"Payroll?" Spence leaned forward.

"Yes. But I told you I have no control of or even access to the books."

Spence held his temper. What is it about accountants, he thought, that limits their world and their imagination to bookkeeping functions?

"Tell me about the payroll. How big is it? How is it met? Cash, coin, or chits? How is it delivered, and from where?"

McLeod was flustered by the questions but began to realize the possibilities created by the direction of his colleague's thinking, and his ordered mind began putting together the operations of the payroll department in meeting the monthly payday of the company's workers.

As McLeod described the inner workings of the company's payroll operation, Spence's mind began working the angles, searching for weaknesses in the system. He identified the potentials, discarding some, keeping others, picking the nuggets from the large amount of gravel McLeod was spilling on the table between them.

McLeod explained the company's relationship with the Mexican banking system, which was mandated by the Díaz regime. He talked about the recent strike, which was a result of the Mexican miners' complaints about being paid in silver pesos while the American miners were paid in gold dollars and how the company had agreed to pay all the miners in dollars. Spence began to sense a bit of optimism as he learned the details from McLeod, and he was particularly pleased to learn that the company's main bank in Mexico was the Banco del Mar in Hermosillo. This made sense because it was the largest bank in northwest Mexico, and when he thought of his long and profitable relationship with the bank and its owner, a small surge of excitement went through him, and his earlier disappointment and frustration began to fade.

Spence learned that the monthly payroll was between two hundred and two hundred and fifty thousand dollars.

Every month, two days before the payroll was shipped, several officers of the company's payroll section came to Hermosillo and attended to all the security details at the bank and railroad. The local military garrison provided an escort from the bank to the rail station, and the company security detail rode with the payroll to Cananea. In all the history of the mine's operation, there had never been an attempt to rob the payroll. The Mexican railroad provided the mining company with a special run to eliminate the necessity for a switch of engines for the route off the main rail line to Cananea. This special run made only two stops: at the railway junction in the town of Benjamin Hill and then at Magdalena, about forty miles further north. McLeod had ridden this train several times and found that the company officials considered the trip to be routine. Under Spence's careful questioning, McLeod remembered the two stops as being short, with no special security provided by the military at either station. The baggage car was locked and manned by a supervisor and two armed security guards, and access to this car was limited to company officers who rode in the adjoining car.

"That would include you?" Spence asked.

"Yes. But the supervisor is very strict about regulations, and I have not seen anyone come or go from the car during the entire trip."

"But would he open up for you if you had a good reason?"

"Well, yes, but it would have to be a very good reason." McLeod was beginning to understand. "Are you thinking of taking it at one of the stops?"

Spence smiled at the accountant's question. He could not picture this man being a part of any violent action.

"Maybe. What about at the bank? Where is the payroll kept, and who has access to it?"

"The payroll is kept in a safe in a secure room just off the safety deposit room and is transferred into two company strongboxes for transport to the mine."

"How heavy are the boxes, and how are they locked?" Spence could feel McLeod warming to the possibilities.

"They don't seem to be that heavy. I've seen two men carry one pretty easily from the bank to the wagon. In fact, I saw one guard carry a box by himself. I would estimate each one to be about thirty to thirty-five pounds. After the money is counted by a payroll bookkeeper, he and the bank official sign the transfer documents. The bank officer puts the money into the boxes, and the senior guard places the company locks and seals on the boxes in full view of the bookkeeper and the banker."

"Who has the key to the padlocks?"

"No one has the key. The locks are brought from the mine without keys, and once the count is complete, they are placed on the boxes and are not opened until they are back at the mine payroll office. Look, the company is not so much worried about bandits as they are about pilferage from inside. They have confidence that the *rurales* and the Mexican army are enough of a deterrent. Besides, Sonora doesn't have a problem with bandits and outlaws like Chihuahua and some of the other states."

"Where are the seals kept?"

"They are also kept in the payroll office, in the same cabinet with the locks."

"When does the counting of the payroll and securing of the boxes take place?"

"The afternoon of the day before the shipment."

"Who at the bank is in charge of putting together the payroll for delivery?"

"I don't know."

"How is the money put up, and what denomination bills are used and how much per bundle?"

"There is nothing bigger than a twenty-dollar bill. There are tens and fives and a small amount of gold and silver coins. The cash is separated into cloth sacks, but I don't know the amount in each."

"What does the security detail do after the business at the bank?"

"They relax. Get something to eat and drink, and some of them seek out other diversions."

Spence sensed a strong note of disapproval in the fussy little accountant's tone. He would get him to tell him more about these diversions later, because if these diversions were sought at the local brothels, there might be a soft spot in the security he could exploit. He always preferred to move against weakness instead of strength. He was quiet for a while and was aware of McLeod looking at him with a desperate confidence.

"I don't know what you have in mind, but I figure I have two, three weeks at the most before I have to be gone, out of Mexico and out of sight for a long time." McLeod's voice was tense.

Spence studied the accountant while he thought about the possibilities. There were two ways of getting the payroll … the violent way or the quiet way. His preference was for the quiet way, and he couldn't accomplish that without McLeod's help. Spence had always had faith in McLeod's talents in the past, but he was no longer confident in the man's judgment. To throw over a carefully planned counterfeit certificate scheme that would have netted them well over half a million dollars for a shortsighted, low-return scheme was unacceptable, and the accountant would damn sure have to buy his way into any new plan. The lack of time to thoroughly create a plan increased the risk but also made the challenge more exciting.

"I need to work on the details, and I need to hire some people I know for the hard part. I need money up front, and since I invested a considerable sum in the certificate operation, which I can't recoup because the plan is now dead, I am short of spare change." He looked directly into McLeod's eyes. "Edgar, not only did you cost me a lot of money, but I just can't bring myself to trust your judgment after what you did. If you want to be part of this, you will have to buy in."

McLeod flushed and looked away. He knew he was fortunate to still be here planning another operation with Spence, and now he had to make himself an intricate part of this plan or walk out of the hotel and immediately begin running. It was no longer the company who was the biggest threat, it was the man sitting calmly across the table from him.

"How much will you need?"

"Twenty thousand," Spence answered calmly.

McLeod's heart sank—the amount Spence demanded was too much. He had about twenty-eight thousand in the bank. He was thinking about the money and how much he would need to get out and start over somewhere and knew that it was not nearly enough. He began exploring other possibilities but quickly realized he had run out of options.

"Come on, Edgar. That's a small percentage of what we can expect to get out of this, and you know that everyone always gets their fair share from me and they get it on time."

McLeod knew that this was true. Spence always paid well and quickly. "That's fine. Count me in. I'll have the money for you tomorrow."

Spence smiled and reached his hand across the table. McLeod took it, and they shook hands. McLeod was still uneasy. He had seen that smile before.

After McLeod left the hotel, Spence walked down the street to the International Telegraph and Telephone office. He had the operator place a call to a number in Mexico City. When the operator signaled that he had Spence's party on the line, Spence picked up the telephone in cubicle number three. "Hello? Yes it's me. The conference on the certificates has been cancelled. What? No, not postponed. Cancelled! I have a new contract." The connection was poor and he had to speak loudly. "The new contract will require the services of our American associates and all their documents. What? Yes, bring all the American documents with you for the meeting." He strained to hear through the crackling on the wire. "Yes, three days from today, and we will need our friend Sir James. Yes. He will participate in the negotiations. So bring him and all of the English newspapers you can get your hands on." The static cleared and the voice from Mexico City came through loud and clear. "Yes. That is all. See you soon."

Spence hummed to himself as he went over to the desk to pay for the call. He was beginning to feel much better about the future.

NINE

C aptain Wheeler was an energetic man and totally committed to the success of the Arizona Rangers. He had moved Ranger headquarters from Bisbee to the crime-ridden town of Naco on the border. He spent much of his time in the saddle, visiting far-flung Ranger posts throughout the territory, and he truly cared for his men, many of whom he had personally selected. Overall, they were steady men, and he relied on them to exercise good judgment as they operated independently and without support in the remotest regions of Arizona. The captain was also a stickler for detail and accountability, so it irritated him that these same rangers who would stay horseback for days on the trail, ignore extreme heat and bitter cold, and go into harm's way without a second thought were so lackadaisical in providing his administrative sergeant the proper receipts and documentation for their expenses. Many of the rangers did a poor job of properly documenting the statements of witnesses and providing a record of their actions in enforcing the law, especially in cases where shooting was involved. He was aware that many of them were not particularly well educated and were actually more fearful of putting pen to paper than facing a desperate lawbreaker, but still.

Owen P. Jones was the exception. The captain never had to ask Jones for receipts, and his written reports were always short, complete, and to the point. He had come to rely a great deal on Jones and was disappointed that Jones had declined several offers of promotion.

Jones now sat with Ashley in wooden straight-back chairs in front of Wheeler's desk in Ranger headquarters. The captain observed the sharp contrast in the two men. Young Ashley could barely control his energy as they discussed the episode of the rustlers at Las Vegas del Oso. Jones sagged in his chair, and the dark circles under his eyes made the captain wonder if he might be pushing one of his best men too hard. After Jones and Ashley brought the captain up to date and Jones handed him his written report, the captain told Ashley to wrap up the details with Sergeant Craig and asked Jones to stay a moment. After Ashley left the small room and the door was closed, the captain got up from his swivel chair and sat on the corner of his desk.

"You feeling OK, Owen?"

"I'm fine, just getting over this cold. Sounds a lot worse than it is."

"You sure?"

"Yep, why the concern, Captain?"

"Because I want you to go to Mexico."

Jones looked at the captain. His eyelids felt very heavy. "Mexico?"

"I've been in touch with Colonel Kosterlitsky, the leader of the *rurales*—you're familiar with the Mexican border police—and I briefed him on the MacDuff women and Mitchell. The colonel tells me that he received word from an informant that Mitchell and his gang were up in the Sierra Madre in the spring. He's not sure where they are now, but he believes they are still in Mexico. He also told me that his source says that there are some Americans with Mitchell.

As soon as he can locate them, he and his *rurales* will mount an operation against the gang, so I suggested to him that with your knowledge of the MacDuff case, you should go down and work with him and his boys. He thought it was grand idea, so you had best rest up and get some decent grub. In the meantime, I'll work out the details with the colonel."

Jones nodded and began to get up from his chair.

"Stay a minute, Owen." Captain Wheeler held up his hand. "Tell me about Ashley. How's he working out?"

Owen leaned against the back of his chair.

"He's workin' out fine, Captain. He was doin' some serious thinking after he shot the rustler, but he came out of it quick. He's young, but he's smart, a quick learner, and he's got good judgment. He'll be fine."

"Glad to hear that, Owen. We'll be needing more like him." The captain went back around the desk and sat in his chair. He leaned back and put his feet up on the desk.

"Time is moving right along, Owen. I would like to see more young'uns like Ashley join up. They seem to be at ease with the new things like written reports, automobiles, telephones, and aeroplanes." He shook his head. "And have you heard about fingerprinting?"

"Yes, but I don't know much about it." Jones's head throbbed.

"It's the latest science in identifying people." The captain took his feet down and leaned forward, his elbows on the desk. "Imagine if we caught somebody in the territory that was wanted, say somewhere back East, and his fingerprints match what the authorities have back there. Hell, we wouldn't even have to have a photograph or drawing of him. Of course, it'll be a while before everything is properly sorted out and organized, not to mention a whole record-keeping system needing to be set up. I reckon that there will be a whole new bunch of lawmen specializing in this science and every department will have their own. Just imagine what a boon it will be for us."

Jones smiled at the captain's enthusiasm, but at the same time, he wondered if the Rangers would be around when this new science came to pass. They both knew that some politicians in Phoenix were working hard to pass legislation to abolish the Rangers, and he was impressed that the captain never discussed the fact that some well-dressed, well-fed politician whose fat ass had never been on horseback had the power to close down their operation. Jones also knew that Captain Wheeler was aware that some of the sheriffs in the territory were in favor of the legislation and admired him even more for his insistence that his rangers continue to work closely with these same sheriffs. He knew several sheriffs who were envious of the Rangers' success and who especially resented the popularity the Ranger Company enjoyed in the newspapers. That same popularity would certainly count for a lot of votes for any sheriff at election time.

The captain had served in every rank in the Arizona Rangers, had killed outlaws, and had been severely wounded in the line of duty. He never asked his men to do something he wouldn't do himself and always put duty above petty politics. At times, the captain's insistence on strict attention to rules and regulations irritated Jones, but Jones's respect for the man never wavered one bit. In Jones's mind, the sheriffs and politicians who favored abolition of the Rangers couldn't carry the captain's boots on their best day.

"I want you to take Ashley with you to Mexico. Teach him what you know." The captain hesitated a moment. "Especially the paperwork," he chuckled. "And even though you will be representing the Rangers while working with the colonel, you'll have to leave your badges here. Now, go get some rest."

"I will, but I also want to ask some questions around town about the MacDuff case. According to Pete, that fellow, name of Spence, split off from the gang and came here to Naco. I want to try and track his movements here in town."

"OK. Let me know what you find." The captain stood.

"Did you talk with Old Man MacDuff?" Jones asked.

"No, I haven't, but I heard that he's in town for a Cattle Association meeting. I'll set it up so we can both talk to him and let you know." He hesitated and then got up from behind his desk. "Owen, you don't have to answer if you don't want to, but I am curious as to why you have always turned down every promotion I ever offered you."

Jones sighed as he stood. "Captain, it's not that I don't appreciate the offers, but I'm happy just riding herd on my own workload. I never had any desire to worry about another man's responsibilities."

The captain nodded and sat down again behind his big desk.

As Jones opened the door, he noticed that Captain Wheeler was already going through the stack of paperwork on his desk.

The captain had before him on his desk the dismissal papers for one of his rangers, who, while drunk, had assaulted a citizen of the town of Bisbee who was sober. He sighed. This was not the first time one of his rangers had acted stupidly, but it was just the kind of behavior that the politicians could use against him. The soon-to-be-dismissed ranger was a Texan. Why, the captain asked himself, was it always a Texan? Many a former Texas Ranger had found a home in Arizona Territory, and they were excellent in the performance of their duties while out on the trail tracking down outlaws and rustlers. They were tenacious in their pursuit of the law breakers and were responsible for the departure of many an outlaw from the territory. Some of these outlaws fled to other parts of the country, but just as many were sent to the hereafter by these hard men. The captain admired the qualities that made them exceptional lawmen but had come to dislike them as a group. They were opinionated and chafed at any discipline except their own, and they absolutely ignored the required paperwork. He had fielded more complaints by citizens and politicians against Texans than any of the other rangers. Not that they were all like that. There were a few like Jones who had the same hard qualities but had better control and judgment in the balance.

The captain picked up the ranger's badge and slowly turned it in his hand, feeling each of the five rounded points on the star. He gave a deep sigh and then, in bold strokes, signed his name to the dismissal document.

Jones found Ashley at Sergeant Craig's desk, briefed him on the trip to Mexico, and then told him to meet him in front of the hotel in two hours. He left the office and walked down the street to his hotel, got his key from the desk clerk, and climbed the stairs to his room. He stretched out on the bed and began planning the investigation that he hoped would shed some light on this character named Spence. He mentally lined up his sources around town and the order in which he would contact them: the bartenders, the telegraph clerk, Mrs. Cameron at her "boarding house," the barber, hotel deskmen, and others. He was thinking of all this when his weariness caught up with him and he fell into a deep, dreamless sleep.

The sound of someone knocking on his hotel door startled him, and his eyes opened fully as his boots hit the floor. He opened the door to find Ashley standing there, looking slightly uncomfortable. The older ranger was irritated that this was the second time Ashley had had to wake him for work. He went back into the room, retrieved his hat, and pinned his badge to the left pocket of his shirt.

He felt better as they stepped out onto the porch of the hotel into the late-afternoon heat. He flexed the fingers of his right hand and felt them move without the dull ache he had had in the cold of the mountains. The sound of an automobile startled him as he stepped off the sidewalk. He stopped to watch it stutter clumsily down the street, leaving a smell of burnt oil and gasoline in its wake.

"You ever ride in one of those machines?" he asked Ashley.

"Yes, back in California."

"Looks dangerous to me."

"Actually, they're kind of fun. Can't wait to get one." Jones looked at the younger ranger as if he had just blasphemed.

"Why would you do that?" he asked.

"Why, it's the way of the future and I—"

"But you need roads for those damn things. We got plenty of trails but precious few roads." He looked at Ashley like a schoolmaster stuck with a student who could not do simple ciphering.

"Oh, they'll build roads. They'll have to, because it's certain that the automobile will replace the horse in the near future." Ashley watched the noisy machine turn the corner.

Jones realized they were going down two different paths and kept the rest of his thoughts on these contraptions to himself. "You ever ride in one of those flying machines?"

"Aeroplanes? No. But my uncle did, and I'm dying to try it." The excitement was clear and bright on Ashley's face. "Yep. You might just do that." Jones chuckled and began crossing the street, satisfied that his witticism had closed the subject.

They walked around town, visiting with Jones's sources, trying to glean some information about Spence. Jones knew his chances were slim, as he had only a name and Precious Pete's description, but he patiently questioned each of his sources. They drew a blank with the telegraph operator, who sent them over to the telephone switchboard, where they also drew a blank. The hotel clerks and saloonkeepers could not tell them anything, but they had better luck at the barber shop on Towner Avenue. The barber told them that a man fitting Spence's description had come into his shop for a haircut back in the spring.

"He had long hair, and I could tell he had been out on the trail for a while because of the condition of his hair. I noticed he had a couple of pieces of sticking plaster on his face, kinda like you do when you try to shave in a hurry, and the part of his face where his whiskers had been was pale while the rest of his face was red from the sun and wind. I just figured he was trying to save the money a shave would cost him. He coulda saved some skin and blood if he'd of let me do it."

"Did you ever see him after that?"

"Nope."

"How short did you cut his hair?" Jones asked.

"About as short as yours and your partner's."

"How was he dressed?"

"He had on a nice worsted suit and a boiled shirt but no collar. That's why I couldn't understand him scraping his face all up to save two bits. A feller could afford that suit could sure afford the price of a shave, don't you think?"

"You're probably right."

Jones was ready to thank the barber and leave when Ashley asked, "Did you notice any accent when he talked?"

"Now you mention it, yeah. He had a real fine voice, and he talked like an educated man. Very polite and cultured, if you know what I mean."

"Did you notice any scars?" Ashley persisted.

"Yes, I did, a small one up here." The barber pointed to his right eyebrow.

"Is there anything else you can remember about this man?" Jones asked.

"No. Not really. Except I wish he would have stayed around and been a steady customer."

"Why's that?"

"'Cause he was a good tipper." The barber studied Jones's face. "That's a mighty close shave you have. You shave yourself?"

"Yep," Jones answered.

"Straight razor or one of them newfangled safety razors?" His professional curiosity was aroused.

"Star Safety. Just like Justice Holmes." Jones smiled.

"Damned things will put me out of business!" The barber turned and began sweeping the cuttings on the floor.

They had even better luck with Mrs. Cameron. She told them that one of her girls bragged about having a "fancy man" who was going to marry her.

"She said he was going to take her back East where his family had a business."

Mrs. Cameron had seen this man briefly on one occasion, and her description of him matched that given by the barber.

"What's the name of this girl?" Jones asked.

"Ramona Sampson, and she was the prettiest of all my girls!"

"Was?" Ashley asked.

"Yes. She left shortly after her man did."

"Did they leave together—did you ever hear his name?"

"Jim Fremantle is how he introduced himself to me. A few days after he left, Mona came in and told me she was going up to Tucson, where she had a sister. So she left."

"Any idea where her man went?" Jones asked.

"No. All I know is that he was here only a day or two. Took some things Mona was holding for him and left."

"What was it she was holding for him?"

"A small trunk, clothes I reckon. The trunk had a big lock on it."

Ashley looked at the older ranger, the excitement of the hunt clear on his face. He turned to Mrs. Cameron. "Do you know if Miss Sampson's sister is, uh, in the same profession in Tucson? Do you know her name or address?"

"No to all those questions, honey." She smiled at the young ranger.

They thanked Mrs. Cameron and walked over to the train station to see if anyone could remember Spence getting on a train, but they drew another blank, so they went back down Dominguez Street and worked their way back to Ranger headquarters. It was quieter now that darkness was settling in, but in a little while, the saloons would be full and a new round of life and misadventure would begin, and Jones knew that some of it would most likely spill out onto the street.

"I'm betting he went to Mexico," Captain Wheeler said. He was looking out the window at the new streetlights down the street near the border crossing.

"Maybe. But if he did, I don't think it likely that he's holed up with Mitchell and his bunch," Jones said.

"You're probably right. But I gotta say, he sure sounds like an interesting character. We'll have to find this Sampson girl, but in the meantime, you and Ashley will be spending some time down in Sonora with the colonel and his muchachos. I'm waiting for a wire from him, but you all be ready to leave day after tomorrow."

They got up to leave.

"Oh, I almost forgot. Make sure you take a decent suit or at least a good jacket and white shirt and tie with you. The colonel likes to put on the dog whenever we visit him, and they're kind of formal affairs, so let's make sure the Rangers are properly represented in Sonora. And by the way, Owen, MacDuff will be here at ten tomorrow morning."

Jones's irritation grew as they walked out of the office. He hated buying clothes and had only ever bought work clothes when he had to. He did not have a "fancy" jacket or white shirt, much less a tie. He became even more irritated as he thought about having to go down to the general store or haberdasher or wherever it was you bought these damn things!

"I have an extra tie or two if you need one," Ashley offered.

Jones stopped in his tracks. "Now what the hell makes you think I don't own a tie?"

Ashley calmly met his scowl. "Do you?" he asked quietly.

Ashley's calmness and his simple question pushed Jones's irritation aside. He definitely needed more rest.

"No, I don't. And I'd appreciate your help in finding a jacket that would be acceptable at a Mexican fandango or whatever it is the colonel has planned."

TEN

·•·◦━━━◆━━━◦·•·

Jones had seen a lot of death in his life and he had a rule about not thinking about it too much. He believed that death was thrust upon him more often than most people, and he resolved that he would not waste his time trying to understand it. Death just happened. Someday it would happen to him. That was his philosophy on death, and he would not expand upon it. But the one thing about death that he did often think about was its association with color. It was the blood, always in various shades of red when he came upon a victim recently shot, stabbed, or sliced. Later the red blood would turn black at about the same time the body turned gray. And there was the blue on the bruised necks of those who were strangled or the bluish-purple on the face of a hanged man, and when he came upon a body that been dead for a long time, there was a greenish tint to the skin.

He called them his dark colors, and at times, he would wake in the night after dreaming of them. It was the one thing about death that stayed with him, and now he was thinking about these colors again as he and the captain talked with MacDuff.

MacDuff was a large man with the serious look of a territorial rancher who had learned to anticipate and then accept some of the harshest lessons nature can teach. It was obvious that he was a sick man. The skin on his face was a dull gray, and there was a yellowish tinge to the bags under his red-rimmed eyes. His breathing rasped in and out of him, and he winced when he moved. There was no spark in his eyes, and they reflected little interest in life. The colors gave away his secret as Jones told the old rancher what he had learned from Precious Pete. Jones did this without going into detail, and as gently as he could, he told the old man that according to Pete, his wife and daughter had been killed by a band of outlaws in Mexico. MacDuff appeared to accept the news in the same manner he had always received bad news; with strength and the acceptance of things beyond his control. When he thanked the rangers for their work and shook their hands, Jones noticed a hint of emotion slip out of this man who was fighting a losing battle with his own body and who was pushing back the pain with every breath.

"If you find my wife and daughter, Captain, I would appreciate you bringing them home for a proper service and burial."

"If we find them, you can count on it," the captain said. Jones and the captain sat quietly after MacDuff left.

There was no need for any conversation. The colors told it all.

ELEVEN

———◆———

J ones had the window seat on the train as they rolled south after leaving Nogales. He would have preferred riding in the mail car, but this was the Mexican railroad, and unlike the Southern Pacific, they did no special favors for rangers. As he watched the flat cattle country pass by, he began thinking about a dream that had taken root in him. Jones was paid three dollars a day and got another dollar for expenses and fifty cents for forage for his horse each day he traveled. He got by on a lot less than that and had saved against lean times that might come his way. He wasn't particularly frugal; he just did not need much to live on and had accumulated nearly three thousand dollars, which he kept in a bank in Phoenix. He had never given a whole lot of thought to the future and had always preferred to face life day to day, but lately he had found himself thinking ahead.

He was perfectly suited to the life of a lawman, and except for the time he had spent working cattle, it was the only life he had really known. Being a lawman included a lot of routine duties, just like ranch work, but when the excitement came, it filled a need in him and made him whole, like a renewed thrill that would never go stale. But Jones was a realist, first and foremost, and he could feel the years building up in him. He also knew that even if the territorial legislature voted down the bill to abolish the Rangers, it would not be long before Arizona was granted statehood and, just like far west Texas, Arizona would finally be settled. And then what? The cities were growing, and along with them, the police and sheriff's forces would expand, and there would be no need for the Rangers. So his thoughts had recently settled on the prospects of getting his own little spread where he could still live life on his own terms. He liked ranch work since it suited his nature; as with lawman work, all he had to do was just show up in the morning and he would be assured of enough work to last until well past sundown.

Several months ago, the captain had mentioned that an old friend planned to sell off some land south of Tucson near the small settlement of Patagonia, in the high grass country of southern Arizona. Jones had visited the area and looked over the property. He was excited about its location and the quality of the grazing and had gone so far as to discuss it with his banker, who assured him that he had enough in his account to put down on a small operation and that the bank would gladly carry the note at a favorable rate. Jones was not yet ready to ask the captain for more details, but he felt closer to that moment each day.

"Were you really a Texas Ranger?" Ashley asked. Jones sighed and turned from the window.

"Yep. I rode with them for some time." He looked Ashley in the eye. "Why do you ask?"

Ashley blushed. "It's not that I'm trying to pry into your business, but I had always read about them and dreamed about joining up when I was a kid."

"But instead you signed up with this outfit?"

"Yes, but ..." Ashley hesitated.

"Well, J.T., you joined a good outfit, and I wouldn't fret none about not being a Texas Ranger."

"Well, why did you leave them?"

Jones shook his head. He never talked with anyone about his life, but he had taken a liking to Ashley and had encouraged the younger man to be open with him, and it was only fair that he do the same.

"I left because the outfit was changing and Texas was changing. When I first joined the Frontier Battalion, there was still plenty of outlaws and Indians raisin' hell in far west Texas and we had our fair share of action. But even before that, the Comanches had been whipped and old Quanah Parker and his bunch were on a reservation. And they had chased old Victorio and his Apaches all over west Texas and down into Mexico, where the Mexicans found them and wiped them out. So when I joined up, there was only a scattering of Victorio's people still raiding. They kept us plenty busy, but it was just a matter of time before we took care of them. Then in my last few years with the outfit, we were dealin' with a few old-time bandidos, bank robbers, and the like, but more and more people moved out from east and central Texas and things began to settle down, and we found ourselves being used for things I found irksome."

"Like what?" Ashley asked.

"Well, like the time they sent us to El Paso to stop the heavy-weight fight between Fitzsimmons and Maher. Hell, I'd have paid good money to see those two fight, but here I was under orders to go to El Paso along with most of the whole battalion and stop the match. The fight never took place, and the Mexicans wouldn't allow them to fight in Juarez either. So old Judge Roy Bean set up the match on a little island in the Rio Grande."

"What happened then?"

"Ruby Bob knocked Pete Maher out in the first couple of minutes of the fight. So I guess I didn't miss much after all."

"So that's it? That's why you left?"

"No. That's not all. A couple of years later, smallpox broke out on the border in south Texas. The doctors were trying to quarantine the infected, who were mostly Mexicans. The Mexicans are real touchy about anybody interfering in family matters, and there was never any love lost between the Mexicans and the Rangers to begin with, but this really brought it to a head. Some of the Mexicans were fighting the doctors taking away their family, and it got pretty heated. There was a shootout, and a Mexican shot one of our captains. We killed that one and shot up close to a dozen more, including some women. It just didn't set right with me, and I got to thinking that if we were going to be used for escorting doctors and the like, well, I didn't want any part of it. So I turned in my badge in El Paso."

"Any regrets?" Ashley asked.

"None." Jones turned to look back out the window.

"How do you feel about Mexicans, Owen? I mean, what with us on our way to work with them and all?"

"Mexicans got their good ones and their bad ones, just like we do."

"Ever been to Mexico before?"

"Yep. But not as far south as we're going."

"Ever work with the *rurales*?"

"No, but I met them once when we turned over a couple of Mexican bandidos just south of Douglas."

"What do you think of them?"

"The *rurales*? Well, they got a reputation of being a real hard outfit. And Mexico has different laws and ways of operating than we do. So the *rurales* sometimes act as judge, jury, and executioner. They got a rule down there they call *ley fuga*, the law of flight. They can shoot anybody trying to escape from their custody. Like I said, a hard outfit. These old boys don't take many prisoners."

"What's their colonel's name? Kosterlitsky?"

"Yep. Cap told me he's a Russian ended up in Mexico as a youngster. Tough old bird. Was an officer in the Mexican army, and now he heads up the *rurales* in northern Mexico. He's one of President Díaz's favorites, and he's also a friend of Captain Wheeler. By the way, you'll hear the *rurales* called the Gendarmería Fiscal. That's their official name." Jones turned to look at Ashley. "Looks like I'm not going to get any sleep on this trip, so let me ask you some questions."

"Sure, Owen. What do you want to know?"

"Why did you join up with the Rangers?"

Ashley took off his hat and put in on his knee. "It was my father. I mean—he had my life planned for me. First college, then medical school, and then he planned for me to join him in his practice."

Jones turned to look at the young ranger with surprise. "Your father is a doctor?"

"Yes. He has a large practice in Los Angeles."

"And you went to medical school?"

"Well, yes, but I left after my second year and came east to Arizona."

"Now why the hell would you do that?" Jones's eyes were wide.

"I wanted to live life on my own. I wanted some adventure, and I heard about the Rangers from my uncle, who is a good friend of the governor and—"

"So that's how ..." Jones trailed off.

"I shouldn't have told you that. Please don't tell anyone."

"It's none of my business, much less anyone else's."

"And then there was this girl and it was all getting too serious, and I could see my life planned for me for the next forty years and I just had to get away."

"This girl? Are you taken with her?"

"Well, yes, but ..."

"But what?"

"Well, I mean, we still correspond, and I want to ..." Ashley was turning a deep red. "Dammit! I just need to live like I want to. Besides, I'm not ready to concentrate on medicine yet. You need one hundred percent commitment for medicine, and I don't have it right now."

Jones sat up straight and looked at Ashley sharply for a moment. "You don't need one hundred percent commitment for this job?"

"Yes, I do. I want this more than anything in my life."

"Including the girl?"

"Yes."

Jones slouched in his seat and tipped his hat down over his eyes.

"What about you, Owen? Do you have a girl?"

Jones sat with his hat covering his face and thought about Ashley's question. He thought about Elizabeth, the waitress at the Alameda Lunch Parlor in Tucson, and her long blond hair that she wore up in the style of all waitresses and how she would take it down so that it flowed over her shoulders to frame a pair of the clearest blue eyes he had ever seen. He thought about the light dusting of freckles on the bridge of her nose and how they seemed to multiply when she laughed. And how, when they would go on picnics in the foothills above Tucson, she would brazenly smoke cigarettes and take off her clothes and wade in the small stream and how she made his heart feel young and made his dark colors fade. And then he thought about going into the Alameda after a long scout on the Verde and being told by one of the other waitresses that Elizabeth had gone off to Denver with a Sears and Roebuck drummer.

"No. There's no girl," he told Ashley.

TWELVE

T he colonel and a detail of two *rurales* met the rangers at the train station in Magdelena. As Jones stepped out of the doors onto the wooden platform, he studied the Mexicans closely. They were clean-shaven with the exception of large cavalry-type mustaches, and all wore light-gray *charro* jackets with matching tight-fitting britches. The silver buttons on their jackets gleamed in the bright sunlight, and their clean white shirts were secured at the neck with black ties. They all wore gray Mexican-style sombreros and long cavalry sabers with brightly polished scabbards. The officers' uniforms were trimmed with silver. The sergeant whose uniform was trimmed with white piping held the reins of two beautiful gray mares, each freshly brushed and wearing a fancy saddle with large Mexican-style pommels. He looked forward to working with these men in the hunt for Mitchell and his gang.

The colonel, a slim, gray-haired man with a gray mustache, dismounted and came over to the rangers. "I am Colonel Emilio Kosterlitsky of the Gendarmería Fiscal. Welcome to Mexico," he announced, holding out his hand.

They shook hands, and the colonel introduced the rangers to his men, Lieutenant Nicolás Holguín and Sergeant Miguel

Montaño. Colonel Kosterlitsky then nodded in the direction of the two mares. "I hope you gentlemen will find these mounts satisfactory. My men will arrange for the delivery of your baggage."

Jones pointed with his rifle to the two grips at their feet. "That's all our baggage, colonel."

The colonel looked at the two small grips and smiled. "Bueno! Shall we go, then?"

Jones had the old feeling of being closed in as they rode through the winding streets of Magdalena. He studied with interest the armament of the *rurales*. Each had a Spanish Mauser secured in a military-style saddle scabbard and wore a Colt revolver high at the waist. Jones's eyes were again drawn to the big sabers as the clinking of the scabbards and attachments echoed in the narrow streets of the town.

After a while, they came out of the narrow streets onto a main street and rode down this wide boulevard until they came to the colonel's hacienda. They rode around to the back, where they were met by a captain and, behind him, a group of stable boys. Jones and Ashley dismounted, and the colonel introduced them to the captain, whose name was Amador. The colonel then pointed to a set of double doors at the back of a large white building.

"In here, gentlemen."

They entered a large, cool room in the center of which was a huge table covered with platters filled with several different meats, all sorts of fresh vegetables and fruit, and at least three types of bread. Carafes of wine and pitchers of water were set at regular intervals down the table. After the men sat, several women began filling their plates with food and pouring wine into the heavy goblets at each place setting. The colonel stood at the head of the table, waited for the wine goblets to be filled, and then called for their attention. The men all stood. The colonel lifted his full wine glass and toasted President Díaz and the republic, and everyone took a sip of wine. He then toasted President Roosevelt and the

United States. They took another sip, and after he toasted the co-operation between the Arizona Rangers and the Gendarmería Fiscal, he drank deeply from his goblet of wine and motioned for the men to be seated. With that, the meal began. Jones was anxious to discuss his search for the killers, but he sensed there would be no business during the meal, so he relaxed as he and Ashley spent the next few hours getting acquainted with the colonel and his officers and talking over general issues of the day in their respective countries. After the table was cleared and the cloth removed, coffee, brandy, and cigars were brought, and when everyone's cups and snifters were filled and the cigars lit, the colonel opened the discussion of their joint venture. Then he asked Jones to brief them on what he knew about the Mitchell gang and their crimes in Arizona.

Jones was impressed with the officer's command of the English language. All except the sergeant spoke the language formally and correctly. Jones laid out details of the gang's criminal activities as well as the intelligence he possessed on the individual members. He told the group about the man called Spence but admitted he did not know the extent of Spence's relationship with Mitchell and his gang. Jones was encouraged by the way the colonel and his men asked questions, and after he answered each of them, he told them what he knew about the kidnapping and murders of the MacDuff women. He described, word for word, in a dispassionate manner, the story told him by Precious Pete, and as he spoke, he became aware of the changing mood at the table. The warmth and camaraderie faded, and the Mexicans' easy smiles were replaced with grim looks. He watched the frowns grow deeper and their eyes take on a malevolent cast as he finished describing the rape and murder of the woman and her daughter. In the long quiet following his tale, Jones's respect for these men grew.

Jones was accustomed to covering his true feelings with a cold professional demeanor, so it interested him that these men apparently shared the same hatred and, possibly, the same despair of evil that he did but they did not restrain any expression of their emotions.

All except Jones sipped at their wine in the silence. He had never drunk wine before, and after the first few sips at this table, he knew he never would again.

"So!" Captain Amador looked at the colonel. The colonel nodded his head, and the captain turned back to Jones. "You would prefer to first visit the location on the river near Bacoachic to find the bodies and corroborate this man Pete's story?"

"Yes I would, Captain. And I would like to do that as soon as possible," Jones answered.

The captain looked at the colonel before speaking again. "We had planned for Lieutenant Holgíun to take a detail to the village of Villanueva to follow up on the information the colonel received yesterday about a fellow named Alberto. The village is not so far from this location on the river."

"Ah, yes! Alberto." The colonel drummed his fingers on the table. "Excellent! We will combine the two tasks, and I believe tomorrow morning would be a good time to start." He turned to Jones. "I have been thinking that if you do find the bodies, you can take them to Cananea. There is a very good doctor there, and I will arrange for him to assist you with any necessary examinations."

"Thank you, Colonel."

The colonel pushed his chair back from the table and crossed his legs. "Good! Now let us enjoy our brandy and cigars, and you can bring me up to date on the life and adventures of my friend Captain Wheeler."

As quickly as they had disappeared, the good spirits and friendly camaraderie returned to the table, and the men all sat talking and drinking brandy late into the night.

THIRTEEN

ilvestre Silva was president of the Banco del Mar. He was a graduate of some of the finest schools in Spain and found his fortune in Mexico's banking system decades ago. He moved easily in the influential social circles of his father, and in fact, it was these connections that made him one of the wealthiest bankers in the north of the Republic. As his father had taught him, he was always in search of a means to grow his business and, like his father, he did not mind bending the rules to do so. His clients were among the richest citizens of Mexico. He also catered to a few choice clients in Europe and the United States who required a discreet bank to hide large sums from the authorities.

The man who sat in one of the leather batwing chairs in his office was one of those clients. This man who everyone called Spence but who was known to Silva as John Stanford had been a client for years. Silva knew that Stanford was not his real name but could not care less because in all his dealings with Stanford, they both always made a nice profit with a minimum of risk.

Silva looked out the windows of his offices onto Hermosillo's central plaza. The people walked under the long shadows of the palm trees; the bootblacks and lottery ticket sellers circled the perimeter of the evening promenade hoping to attract buyers for their wares. They moved quickly around the stately pace of the evening promenade.

"I will need to deposit a significant amount in dollars and will need to transfer a large portion of funds to my account in your Mexico City bank."

"Of course! When will you require the transfer?"

"Within the week."

Silva turned from the window and rubbed his hands together. He was accustomed to Stanford transferring large amounts of money in various currencies in and out of his bank, and Silva was always well compensated for his discretion as well as his studious disregard for the required forms and receipts. Silva suggested they continue their business over champagne and canapés across the street at Stanford's hotel. He grabbed his hat from the rack and led the way out of his offices.

Spence spotted her as he entered the main lobby of the hotel. She was with her husband and an older couple, and they were all dressed for an evening at the opera. Silva followed Spence's gaze and was amused when Señora del Castillo waved and called out, "Mr. Stanford!"

A look of annoyance quickly crossed her husband's face, but he came over and shook Spence's hand and said hello to Silva. The group engaged in small talk for a few minutes, during which Mrs. del Castillo studied Spence closely.

"Will you join us in glass of champagne?" Spence asked.

"Unfortunately, we cannot join you. Perhaps another time." Señor del Castillo smiled.

"You are not going to opening night, Silvestre?" Her eyes sparkled.

"Business, I'm afraid." Silva shrugged his shoulders.

"You work too hard, Silvestre," Señor del Castillo's voice boomed.

Silva smiled. You should know, you old pirate, he thought.

Spence and Silva watched as the foursome walked out of the hotel.

"Come, Mr. Stanford. The champagne awaits!" Silva said with a chuckle.

They sat at a table, ate oysters on the half shell, and drank champagne while Spence explained how he had met the del Castillos on the train.

"Who is he?" Spence asked.

Silva signaled the waiter for another platter of oysters. "He is a lawyer, an influential *hacendado*, a friend of the governor, one of our best clients, and someone you want to avoid."

"Interesting. Tell me more."

"There is nothing more you need to know, except that he keeps a suite of rooms here at the hotel for when he is in town." Silva leaned back and cocked his head at Spence. "However, I am convinced it is not him but his wife that interests you, no?"

Spence smiled and sipped his champagne. Silva leaned across the table and waved his finger back and forth.

"Let me tell you, my friend, she is every bit the shark he is. *Mucho cuidado*, eh?"

Several days later, del Castillo stood at Silva's window and looked across the street to the plaza.

"Do you have the information on the Englishman I asked about? The associate of John Stanford?" he asked Silva.

"My colleagues in the capital verified it yesterday through their contacts in the British embassy. His name is Sir James Westford, an intimate of the royal family and a decorated war hero. He lost his eye and was wounded in the leg during the English war in

Africa. He represents English mining interests and is trying to establish a shipping link here in the north."

Silva sat at his desk, going through several telegrams. "Tell me again how you met?" he asked del Castillo.

"He was with that man Stanford in the restaurant at the hotel. Stanford introduced us and told me that the *inglés* was in need of a Mexican lawyer here in Hermosillo to assist in this shipping business thing. How would Stanford know him?" He turned from the window and faced Silva.

"I know Stanford to be an influential businessman and a lawyer who represents several companies in New York and San Francisco that have had long-standing relationships with our bank both here and in the capital. So it's not surprising that he and the Englishman may have had or still have mutual business interests."

"But doesn't it seem odd that this lawyer Stanford wouldn't know a Mexican lawyer? Or that the British embassy wouldn't provide legal representation for a friend of their royalty here in the republic?"

"Perhaps, but to my knowledge, Stanford has never had any connection with a law firm here in Mexico. He has never had the need for one as far as I know." Silva got up and walked over to the bar. "A sherry, Señor del Castillo?"

Del Castillo shook his head impatiently.

"Two other things occur to me." Silva said as he poured a small measure of sherry. "One is that Americans are very informal in how they conduct their business, and the second is that this may be an independent venture, if you know what I mean. Perhaps 'off the books,' as the Americans say."

"Perhaps," del Castillo frowned.

"If you have any doubt, perhaps you should turn him down." Silva sipped lightly at the sherry.

"Yes, exactly. Well thank you, Silvestre." del Castillo took his hat from the table and walked out the door, leaving it wide open.

Silva went over and closed the door then took his glass over to the window and looked out at the hotel. Now what was that gringo up to? Well, he had given him fair warning. He looked at the plaza, a square of brightness in the evening shadows, and began to consider how he might squeeze out a commission from this business between Stanford, the Englishman, and that old pirate del Castillo.

FOURTEEN

L ieutenant Holguín signaled the column of riders to a halt as they rounded the last bend in the narrow trail at the point just before it began its descent into the valley of Villanueva. Holguín rode in the Mexican style, high and straight in the saddle, and he looked as fresh as he had in the early morning when they began their journey. The rangers, who rode immediately behind Holguín, looked out over the large valley. The village sat at the edge of a small river that ran down from the hills in the east and was surrounded by fields broken up into squares of various shades of green. The midday sun reflected off the twin towers of the church that stood out above the collection of low white buildings. The lieutenant called for Sergeant Montaño and pointed to one of the outlying ranches. Jones heard him tell the sergeant to take four men and to "go see about Alberto." The sergeant and his men rode back up the trail and made a long circuitous approach to the valley and the ranch to which Holguín had pointed. The main column then proceeded down the trail and rode across the valley to the village, where the mayor and the priest met them in the plaza across the street from the church. The men dismounted and enjoyed the cool shade under the cottonwoods of the plaza. After Holguín introduced the rangers, the mayor invited them into the municipal building for lunch.

A simple meal was laid out for them on a large, bare table that also served as the mayor's desk. While they ate, the mayor brought the lieutenant up to date on the current events in the village and the valley. Things had been quiet with no trouble from bandits, there had been an abundant crop this year, and overall, the mayor was very pleased with conditions. There was, however, a matter of some delicacy that was causing a lot of gossip and some discontent among the people, and much to the mayor's regret, the circumstances of this affair were beyond his authority and jurisdiction. He hoped that the lieutenant could mention this matter to the colonel, who could then provide the mayor with some suggestion for a solution. Lieutenant Holguín looked at Jones.

"Can you and Juanito understand if we continue in Spanish?" The lieutenant asked. The *rurales* had some trouble pronouncing the initials J.T. and had decided to call Ashley "Juanito."

"Yes," Jones answered for both of them.

The lieutenant turned back to the mayor and asked him to describe in detail this delicate matter he had begun discussing. The mayor sighed and made the proper regrets and apologies for burdening the lieutenant with matters that, although scandalous, were civil and not criminal in nature. He then went on to explain that there was a farmer in the valley who was well respected for his ability to produce a profitable crop year after year, as well as his ability to have produced three of the most beautiful daughters in the valley. He was an influential man among the people and had been of great assistance to the mayor in several civil matters that could have easily escalated to unrest and even violence.

Although the farmer enjoyed a good reputation and was well respected in the valley, the basis of his real pride was his wife and daughters. The oldest girl was married to a young ambitious farmer, and the youngest was still a child. It was the middle daughter who was the center of the scandalous matter. She had been having a secret relationship with the son of the wealthiest *hacendado* in the valley, which had unfortunately resulted in her becoming pregnant. The mayor admitted that these things happened and were usually resolved with some sort of accommodation by the family of the boy. In this case, however, the *hacendado*, who owned one of the largest ranches in the region, was a very powerful and arrogant man. He refused to even discuss the matter with the mayor and the priest. To make matters worse, the *hacendado* had made comments in public that the farmer should keep his hens locked up and away from the roosters in the valley. This had caused much discontent among the people in the valley and every day the stain on the farmer's honor grew. The mayor and the priest were convinced that the farmer would take the only action left to salvage his honor.

"You can only imagine the consequence of such action," the priest said.

Lieutenant Holguín sat quietly for a moment. "It is certain that the son of the *hacendado* is the party responsible for her predicament?" he asked the mayor and the priest.

"Clearly," said the mayor.

"Without doubt," added the priest.

"What is the boy's name, and where is the ranch?" Holguín asked.

After the mayor provided the name and directions to the ranch, the lieutenant went to the door and called for his corporal. He instructed the corporal to take four men and go to the ranch and bring the young man back under guard, and that if the rancher gave any resistance, he was to be placed under arrest and brought along also. Then the lieutenant turned to the priest. "Father, I suggest you go and bring your proper vestments." He then turned to the mayor. "Can you have the farmer and his daughter come here, or should I send men for them as well?"

"No need, *Teniente*! I will have them here shortly." The mayor seemed very relieved to have this unpleasantness off his hands.

Lieutenant Holguín and the rangers walked out of the building and down the street to the stables where their horses were being fed and watered. The lieutenant's horse came over to the fence and put his head over the top rail when he saw them approach. Holguín ran his hand up the horse's jawline and scratched lightly under the horse's ear. "Do you often get involved in civil matters?" he asked the rangers.

"No, not very often," Jones replied.

"Here in Mexico, we make every effort not to; however, as you can see, this little matter of the heart will no doubt lead to something much worse, and it will be the farmer who goes to prison. This would only cause more discontent among the people, and who knows what would then happen. No! It is better to address these matters quickly at the beginning. You have an expression, something about stitching?"

"A stitch in time saves nine," Ashley replied.

The sound of horses coming down the street and the metallic clinking of saber attachments and other equipment told them that Sergeant Montaño and his men had returned. They left the stables and walked over to the plaza to watch as the sergeant and his squad approached. The sergeant was in the lead as his men followed, surrounding a sixth man whose hands were tied in front of him and who wore only his trousers. A loaded pack mule trailed behind the last man. As the squad dismounted, the lieutenant walked over to their prisoner.

"Hello, Alberto!"

"Hello, Lieutenant." The prisoner's eyes made brief contact with him before immediately looking back down.

Sergeant Montaño carried a *rurales* uniform over to the lieutenant.

"And the sombrero?" the lieutenant asked, still looking at the prisoner.

"He says he sold it," the sergeant answered.

"I hope you got a fair price for it, Alberto." The lieutenant handed the uniform back to Sergeant Montaño. "And the mule?" he asked.

"Since he left us, it seems that Alberto has been smuggling goods from the United States." The sergeant smiled.

"Come, Alberto. Let us have a drink, and you can tell us all about your adventures."

Holguín asked the rangers to come with him, and they went back into the municipal building and sat at the table. The sergeant sat next to the prisoner, and his men stood behind. The lieutenant poured fruit juice for them all and asked one of the men to bring a bottle of mescal. After the bottle was brought and Holguín filled the prisoner's glass, he began his questioning.

The rangers learned that the prisoner, Alberto, was recruited into the *rurales* two years ago while he was in prison, where he had been incarcerated for robbery. Jones knew that some of the *rurales* had criminal pasts and it was common practice in Mexico to draft these men because of their knowledge of criminals and their activities in the territory. Most of them remained on the right side of the law, but some, like Alberto, went back to their old ways. Jones had observed the same thing in the Ranger outfits in Texas and Arizona. Some men with criminal minds stayed criminals even though they wore a badge or, in this case, a uniform, and when the chance presented itself, they crossed back over to the life of an outlaw. Jones could never see the sense in it, but then, he never spent much time thinking about the workings of a criminal mind; he had enough on his plate just dealing with

the actions of those minds. The lieutenant had explained earlier
to the rangers that one day, Alberto had simply disappeared from
camp and they had later discovered that he had gotten drunk
and, while still wearing his uniform, entered a store in a small
village, taken all the cash the owner had, and discharged his pistol
into the air several times. One of the bullets had ricocheted from
a steel bracket in a ceiling beam and struck the storekeeper's sleeping infant in the head, killing her instantly.

Alberto talked quite freely and appeared at ease among his old
comrades. He told them that after the regrettable incident at the
store, he had headed north to the border and begun smuggling
goods into Mexico from the United States.

While Alberto told his old compadres about his outlaw life,
the lieutenant removed a folded piece of paper from his pocket
and studied it carefully. He then interrupted Alberto's story. "I
have here a figure of five hundred and sixty-seven pesos. Is this
the amount you stole from the store?"

"I cannot remember exactly, Lieutenant, but that sounds correct, more or less."

"And do you have this money?"

"Just the two hundred pesos Sergeant Montaño took from me.
The rest is tied up in the goods on the mule."

"And what are those goods?"

"I have American tobacco, tinned meat, some soap, and ammunition."

"And what were you going to do with the ammunition?" The
lieutenant slowly refolded the piece of paper and placed it back
into his pocket.

"Sell it to some men I know." Alberto would not look at the
lieutenant.

"Who? Bandidos?"

"Yes. Some men living high in the Sierras."

Jones felt his pulse quicken. He looked at Holguín. "Are any of these men named Mitchell?" the lieutenant asked.

"I don't know anyone by that name. I only know a man called Mocho."

Jones sat up straight when he heard the name from Precious Pete's story and nodded to Holguín. "Alberto," the lieutenant said, "can you tell us how to find this Mocho and the others?"

"Yes! But I was supposed to go there two weeks ago and I did not."

"Why not?"

"I was afraid they would take my goods and shoot me."

"Without doubt, a wise decision on your part. Now, help me draw a map to this place of Mocho and his friends."

After Alberto helped with the map and answered, as best he could, all of their questions, the lieutenant called for the mayor and spoke to him in private. The mayor hurriedly left the room, and the lieutenant poured another glass of mescal for Alberto. The lieutenant then ordered several of the men to unload the pack mule and bring the goods into the building. Lieutenant Holguín had his men separate the ammunition from the other goods, and then they all sat at the table, smoking and drinking fruit juice, while Alberto drank more mescal and smoked a cigar that one of his old compadres had given him. They talked more about Alberto's knowledge of criminals and their activities in northern Sonora. Alberto, without any reservation, gave them enough information to locate several badly wanted outlaws and identified people who were sympathetic and helpful to these men. While they talked, Alberto rolled a cigarette and placed it behind his right ear.

The mayor then entered the room with a man he introduced as a merchant who owned the village's only dry goods store. The merchant's eyes lit up when he saw the stack of Alberto's goods on the table.

The merchant looked at the lieutenant. "I can only afford to buy eight hundred and fifty pesos worth of these goods," he said.

"Fine. Do you have the money?" the lieutenant asked. "Surely, mi capitán." The storekeeper reached into his pocket and laid the bills on the table.

"Sergeant! Make sure this gentleman does not take advantage of our good nature."

After the merchant took his goods from the room, the lieutenant ordered Sergeant Montano to set aside some tinned beef, tobacco, and all the ammunition and then distribute the remaining goods among the men. He then combined Alberto's pesos with those of the merchant, counted out seven hundred, and gave the rest to Sergeant Montaño.

"Keep what is appropriate and divide the rest among the men."

Jones watched this transaction with growing concern. Was the lieutenant going to keep this money?

After the sergeant put the money in his shirt pocket, Lieutenant Holguín turned to Alberto and gave a short sigh. "Well, Alberto, let's go then."

They all walked out into the bright afternoon sun, and Jones was surprised to see what appeared to be every citizen of the village standing in and around the plaza. The sergeant cleared a path through the crowd as he and his squad marched Alberto across the plaza to a high adobe wall. The lieutenant stepped onto the small bandstand in the middle of the plaza. The crowd was quiet as he pointed to Alberto.

"This man stole money from a hardworking citizen of the republic in a village close by and killed an innocent child as well. He did this while wearing the uniform of the Gendarmería Fiscal. His crime and the dishonor he brought upon the men who are sworn to uphold the law is unacceptable. All of you will bear witness to the consequences of these acts." He then stepped down from the bandstand and went over to Sergeant Montaño, who stood next to a firing squad of five *rurales*.

The lieutenant took a bandanna from the sergeant and walked over to Alberto, who stood at the wall. His hands were tied behind his back, and he had the look of a man resigned to his fate. He leaned toward the lieutenant and said something Jones could not hear. The lieutenant took the cigarette from behind Alberto's ear and put it in the prisoner's mouth. Holguín lit the cigarette, then walked back to the men and stood quietly as Sergeant Montaño inspected the firing squad's weapons. Alberto watched them go about their business with no particular interest. He puffed heavily on the cigarette, closing one eye against the smoke, thinking of the times he had served on firing squads and suddenly remembering what a poor marksman he had been. He then watched as the lieutenant walked back over to him. He spit out the cigarette.

"Ready, Alberto?" Holguín asked.

"Yes, my lieutenant! Ready!"

Holguín placed the bandanna over Alberto's eyes and tied a firm knot at the back of the man's head. He then turned and walked back to the firing squad. In the dead quiet of the plaza, Jones heard Sergeant Montaño draw his saber from its scabbard. It was a slow, sharp slice of metal on metal, and it set the ranger's teeth on edge.

"*Listos!*" The squad brought their rifles up to their shoulders as the sergeant raised his saber.

"Shoot well, *cabrónes!*" Alberto yelled in a tight voice.

"*Apunten!*" The sergeant checked the squad one final time and then turned toward the condemned man.

"*Fuego!*" The crash of the rifles swept through the plaza, and the villagers flinched, instinctively closing their eyes.

Lieutenant Holguín drew his sidearm as he walked over to Alberto, who had turned and fallen to his right, face-down in the fine powdered dust at the foot of the adobe wall. Alberto lay in the dust and moaned as the lieutenant held his pistol at arm's length and fired. The bullet crashed into the back of Alberto's skull, and the man's moaning stopped. The plaza was quiet. The mayor dismissed the crowd with a silent gesture of his arms. It was if he did not want to disturb the stillness of the plaza with words. The villagers drifted away like ghosts in the heat, and those closest to the adobe wall could just make out a buzzing noise as the flies began to gather and circle around Alberto.

FIFTEEN

"Outrageous!" the *hacendado* snorted. He sat with his son opposite the farmer and his daughter. Lieutenant Holguín presided at the head of the mayor's table. Jones and Ashley watched with amused detachment from the far end of the long table, where they sat with the mayor and the priest.

"Outrageous, señor? In what manner do you speak of outrage?" Holguín's voice was calm and polite.

"This, this …" The rancher waved his arms and sputtered.

"No, señor. The outrage lies in your son taking advantage of your position and a young girl's innocence, and then turning his back on his responsibility. That, señor, is the outrage." The lieutenant spoke in an even voice.

The rancher's son and the girl looked down at the table, their faces radiating a distinct impression of guilt so that not a single man in the room had any doubt of their relationship. The rancher sensed this and abandoned his plan to claim innocence on the part of his son, whom he considered a weakling for not holding up his head at this table of inferiors.

The *hacendado* was not accustomed to being addressed in this manner, and he was incensed that he was forced to sit at the table with this peasant, the mayor, and that damn trouble-making priest, all of whom were always looking for ways to get at his money. But it was apparent to him that this policeman had every intention of carrying on with this farce. Very well, he thought, this is the way it always is. This policeman and the rest could only be manipulated with money. So be it. He softened his tone.

"Perhaps if you and I had a moment of privacy, some sort of accommodation could be reached."

"Perhaps that is possible," Lieutenant Holguín said.

The priest and the mayor shared a look of confusion; the farmer wore a cynical smile.

The lieutenant ordered the four *rurales* at the door to wait with the civilians in the next room. He asked Sergeant Montaño and the rangers to stay.

This is more like it, thought the rancher.

"Now, señor, what would you consider a fair accommodation?" Holguín asked the rancher.

"A thousand pesos sounds more than adequate to me," the rancher replied.

The lieutenant sat back in his chair with an exaggerated sigh of disappointment. "Please, señor. You have seen the number of men in my charge. I would lose all respect. No, we must do better."

The *hacendado* fully expected serious negotiations over the final figure, and this damned policeman proved him right so that when they finally settled on three thousand pesos, the rancher was just glad to have done with this matter.

Jones watched as the rancher handed a stack of bills to Lieutenant Holguín, who then counted out the notes and put them into his jacket pocket. It was beginning to appear that the lieutenant was taking money that was not his. The ranger long ago had accepted the fact that things were different here in Mexico, and although this was getting close to the edge, he knew there was nothing he could do and decided that he would just watch as this thing played out.

"Very well, señor, now that it is settled, I want you to listen to me closely." Holguín leaned over the table and looked the rancher in the eye. "You will agree to the arrangements made here today, and if, in the future, I learn that you have not honored our agreement, I and my men will return, and you will not enjoy our visit. I know that you are, right now, thinking of your friends with much influence in the capital, and it is only natural that you would. And I know that the influence you are considering using is, without doubt, very effective in working with political or administrative action. But I work in a world of more direct action, and all the influence you ever had or will have in the future will never affect me or my actions. Understood?"

The rancher nodded. He had encountered a few wild men in his life and found that it was best to agree with them for the time being and work out the details later.

"Excuse me, señor, I did not hear!" The lieutenant stood.

"Yes! I agree." The rancher fought to keep his temper.

Everyone was called back into the room, and Jones watched with amusement as Lieutenant Holguín presided over the briefest wedding ceremony he had ever witnessed. After the ceremony, the rancher turned his back on everyone and stormed out of the room.

The lieutenant dismissed everyone except his sergeant, the rangers, and the father of the bride. He studied the farmer a moment before speaking. "The *hacendado* is a very proud man, as are you, señor. And because you are an honorable man, I know without doubt that you will understand what I am about to tell you."

The farmer looked at the lieutenant with little interest. "You see," Holguín continued, "the *hacendado* shares the shame caused by his son and told me that he has been looking for a way to make things right. Unfortunately, he felt confined by his place here and, well, you know how things are."

The farmer knew the lieutenant was not speaking the truth, but his cunning told him to listen with respect because sometimes one had to take the long way around and perhaps bend the truth to reach a successful conclusion. He nodded and waited patiently for the lieutenant's solution.

"The *hacendado* felt he could not approach you directly and offer an accommodation. He feared you would not accept, and with both of you being honorable men, well, who knows where that might have led, so he asked me to act as intermediary and request that you consider his offer. But before I ask, and in the condition that you accept, you must agree to never take action that would cause me and my men to come back and resolve things in a simpler manner. Understood?"

The farmer nodded. "Clearly. Yes, Capitán."

"The other condition that we must agree upon is that you never tell anyone the terms of the agreement."

"On my honor, Capitán." The farmer was patient.

Lieutenant Holguín reached into his jacket pocket and took out the three thousand pesos, counted it out, note by note, and stacked the notes on the table. The farmer looked down at the money and then back up to the lieutenant. He hesitated a moment and then, his face an impassive mask, took the notes and put them into his pocket. Without saying a word, he shook hands with the lieutenant, nodded to the others, and walked out of the room.

As the *cordada* of *rurales* rode out of the village, the streets were completely empty of people. The sun was low over the western hills, and in the shadows of late afternoon, the village seemed even more deserted. The north road was a long, slow-climbing grade to the foothills, and while it was still light, they stopped to make camp in a small apple orchard. After unsaddling his horse and seeing to his equipment, Jones walked over to the edge of the orchard and looked out over the valley. It was spread out like a pleasant dream; the small cultivated plots were turning a dark green as the shadows grew toward the eastern slope of the Sierras.

Lieutenant Holguín walked over and stood next to Jones.

"The colonel knew where Alberto was," Jones said without turning. It was more a statement than a question.

"Yes. The colonel has many friends who tell him things, and none of us know how he gets his information. For a while I thought it was the mayor, but now I don't think so."

They stood for a while longer and watched as the lights of the village grew brighter in the shadowed light. A small breeze brought the bittersweet smell of apples rotting on the orchard floor. Holguín turned and started to walk back to the campsite.

"What I don't understand," Jones said, "is how you could let that *hacendado* go on thinking that you are corrupt."

Holguín came over, stood next to Jones, and looked down into the valley. "When you look down there, what do you see?" he asked Jones.

"What?" Jones was puzzled.

"As you stand here and look back, what do you see?" The lieutenant pointed down into the valley.

"Well, I see one of the prettiest little valleys I have ever laid eyes on." Jones looked at Holguín.

"Yes," the lieutenant agreed. "I also see its beauty. But I see something else. I see its fragility."

Jones listened patiently.

"Everyone in the valley plays a role in maintaining the stability of a fragile structure. Some have more influence on its stability than others, but nevertheless, what I mean, Owen, is that the rancher's opinion of me is of no importance. As a man of influence in the valley as well as in all of Sonora, he has certain obligations. He chose to ignore some of these obligations, and by doing so, he weakened the structure. I am sworn to keep the peace and cannot allow his indulgence. I don't give a damn for the rancher's opinion of me. It is only important that he meet his obligations. And if he does so through fear of the colonel and me, then what does it matter as long as he meets them?" He shrugged his shoulders. "Alberto also did not meet his obligations. Imagine what the citizens would think if I addressed the matter of Alberto and ignored that of the rancher and the farmer. No." He shook his head. "Without their trust, there can be no real peace. And without their trust, the dreams of the troublemakers in the republic will come true." Holguín stood silent for a moment and then walked back to the campsite, leaving Jones alone, still looking down at the farms and small ranches as darkness finally covered the valley.

SIXTEEN

⸺◆⸺

T he next morning they started early, and just before noon
they entered another small village. Jones watched the
lieutenant and sergeant dismount without a word and
enter a small building on the main street. As they waited,
Jones studied the buildings on the street. They were identical—
plaster over adobe wearing a thin coat of whitewash—and they all
seemed to be leaning into each other. A group of small children
gathered across the street and watched without expression as the
rurales checked their equipment and drank from their canteens.
After a while, Lieutenant Holguín came out of the building with
an older man and a young woman dressed in black holding the
hand of a small boy. Lieutenant Holguin walked over to Alberto's
mule, took the reins, and led the animal over to the man and
woman. He handed the reins to the man, who stood very straight
with much dignity, and in full view of the column, the lieutenant
reached into his vest pocket and removed the roll of bills he had
taken from Alberto. The lieutenant handed these to the man, and
they exchanged a few words. The man and woman stood in front
of their store and watched as the men mounted and formed into
a riding column. As the column passed by them, the man lifted

his hand and made the sign of the cross. When they had ridden past the last building in the village, Lieutenant Holguín turned to Jones. He motioned back with his thumb.

"The storekeeper Alberto robbed."

Jones nodded. He was chagrined when he remembered his thoughts about Holguín and the money in the mayor's office. He was not sure that he would ever understand how the Mexicans operated, but he had a grudging respect for the simple efficiency of their ways. They rode on, and as they got nearer to the place that Precious Pete had described, Jones became anxious.

They found the spot on the river in the middle of the afternoon. They rode over to the bend in the river and Jones spotted the trees that Precious Pete had described. They shaded a pretty little glade above the bank of the river. He fought against the image that formed in his mind, re-creating the awful day in Pete's words, and he concentrated on locating the burial site. All the men dismounted, and Jones and Ashley walked the ground as the *rurales* led their horses to the shade of the cottonwoods. Lieutenant Holguín and Sergeant Montaño walked on the rangers' flanks, and after covering a short distance, Montaño called them over to where he stood. The soil was a slightly different color, and the weeds and grass less mature than that of the surrounding terrain. Jones measured the distance from the tree with his eyes and nodded.

"This is it," he said.

Sergeant Montaño called for his men to bring the shovels. The lieutenant nodded in agreement when Jones insisted that he and Ashley do the digging. The men seemed relieved to not have to take part in this ghoulish exercise.

Jones and Ashley found part of a body after digging down about four feet. They carefully removed more earth and small rocks, and after working for more than an hour, they had removed all that remained of the bodies. There were still small bits of flesh on the skeletons, but all the connecting tissue had long since decayed, and most of the grayish, parchment-like material that had once been skin sloughed off and fell away so that all they had were the bones. The Sonoran desert had long ago absorbed every bit of liquid from the bodies. The rangers wrapped the bones separately in two canvas bags and loaded the bags on one of the pack mules.

The men of the *cordada* watched the rangers take the remains carefully from the ground and gently, almost reverently, place the bones in the sacks. Several of the older men came over to help tie the canvas bags to the pack frames on the mule. After the sacks were secured to the frames, Jones walked over to the trees, and Ashley watched as he appeared to be looking for something on the ground. Jones stopped and knelt down next to the undergrowth where a small bit of wicker material was stuck on the lower branches of a bush. He carefully removed it, turning the shattered remnants of a picnic basket over in his hands.

"We ate their picnic lunch that was in the basket." Pete's words echoed in the peaceful little glade.

Jones stood and looked back toward the river and saw the *rurales* forming up, preparing to leave. He walked over to his horse, put the pieces of the basket into his saddle bag, and swung himself up into the saddle. The sergeant's orders to the men came to him from a distance, for Jones was in a place far away. He was at a place of reckoning, where his only hope was the promise he held, and he rode apart from the others, holding tight onto his promise. Without it, he was nothing. Without it, he was a man of no consequence.

Ashley and the other men watched guardedly as Jones rode alone on their flank. His face was a harsh mask, his eyes fixed on the horizon. The men in the column who had dealt with hard men and death in its many forms recognized Jones's look as one of terrible resolve, and they were quiet in a way they would have been at a funeral in the presence of one who grieved over the loss of a loved one.

Ashley turned in the saddle and looked back at the burial site to see the full branches of the cottonwoods swaying lightly in a gentle breeze.

The group rode into Cananea and passed through the outskirts of Ronquillo on their way to the large mining company hospital. The rangers looked at the grand houses on either side of the street and nodded to Americans who stopped and stared at two of their countrymen riding with the *rurales*. As the rangers and *rurales* rode up to the front of the hospital, a crowd of men and women, both Mexican and American, had gathered to watch the grim, dust-covered column of men.

Sergeant Montaño remained with the men as they dismounted and saw to the unloading of the remains as the lieutenant and the rangers went into the hospital to find the doctor. As they opened the front door of the clinic, they almost collided with a well-dressed fat man clutching what appeared to be a bottle of medicine to his ample belly. He mumbled an apology and hurried out the door. Jones saw the pale, pinched face of a dysentery victim and noted how the poor fellow looked completely out of place in Cananea.

Dr. Fermin Lovato was a young man and a graduate of Harvard Medical School. He welcomed the lieutenant and the rangers into his office and sat at his desk with a serious look on his face as they told the story of the MacDuff women. He told them that he had gotten word from the colonel to expect them, and he reached into his desk drawer, pulled out a sealed envelope, and handed it to Lieutenant Holguín.

"This arrived on the morning train. Now, how can I help?"

Lieutenant Holguín turned to Jones. "Please," he said.

"Well, to begin with, I need to know for a fact that the remains are female, and I need an approximate age for each. If you can say for certain that their deaths were caused in the manner described by the witness, it will verify what he told me and help build a criminal case for the prosecutor." Jones turned to Ashley. "One more thing. My partner here has had some medical training, and I would appreciate it if you would allow him to be present during your examination of the remains."

"Of course." The doctor looked at Ashley with curiosity. "Lieutenant, please have your men bring the remains around to the building behind this one. That is where I will conduct the examination." Doctor Lovato stood and nodded to Ashley.

The doctor and Ashley left the office by the back door, and after Holguín gave orders for delivery of the remains, he sat down at the doctor's desk and opened the envelope. He read the one-page letter and then went over to the front door and called for Sergeant Montaño. Then the lieutenant came back and laid the letter on the desk.

He told Jones, "The colonel has received word that Mitchell and his gang are camped in the Sierras near a small village where we have some friends. They have been getting supplies in the village and, so far, have been peaceful, but the village chief says they are very bad men and has no doubt they will not remain peaceful for long. I know this village well, and the chief is a good man who can be trusted. It is near the location Alberto said he was to meet the man called Mocho."

Sergeant Montaño came into the room, and Holguín explained the contents of the letter and his desire to send a small party to perform a discreet reconnaissance in the vicinity of the village. The scouting party would send word back when the gang was located and await the arrival of the lieutenant and a larger force of *rurales*. The sergeant and his men were to dress in civilian clothes and travel lightly, with no pack animals. The colonel had already notified the army in the north to be alert for the gang should they try to make a run for the U.S. border.

Holguín turned to Jones and raised his eyebrows.

Jones handed a piece of paper to the sergeant. "Here is a list of names of the gang members I want. I am very interested in learning if any of these men left the gang and where I might find them."

Sergeant Montaño left the room to pick his men for the mission. As he opened the door, a very pretty nurse stood there. The sergeant stood back and held the door as the nurse, with a quick glance at the hard-looking man, came into the room.

"Lieutenant, the chief doctor is here to see Dr. Lovato, but when he learned you were here, he insisted on seeing you."

"What is it he wants?" Holguín asked politely.

"He would not say." Her manner made it clear that the doctor was a man of importance.

"Please send him in," he said. As the nurse started to turn to leave, he added, "and thank you." Holguín smiled at her.

Jones noticed the nurse smile as she left to get the doctor. Very shortly, a large man with a small moustache and carefully combed hair and wearing an expensive suit entered the room and demanded, "Where is Dr. Lovato?"

"He is busy at the moment, assisting us in a serious criminal matter. Excuse me, señor, I was not told your name." Holguín spoke very politely, almost apologetic in his tone.

"I am Doctor Juan Lopez de la Garza, chief medical officer in this district."

Holguín introduced himself and Jones to the doctor.

"I demand to know why I was not consulted in this matter and who instructed Dr. Lovato to conduct an examination without my approval."

"Señor Doctor, please sit down." Holguín gestured to a chair. "I sincerely apologize for this misunderstanding, but the arrangements were made before I arrived. Even so, I should have ensured that you were notified."

Some of the stiffness went out of the doctor. He looked at both men. "And another thing," his voice was not as confrontational as before, "I understand that several bodies have been disinterred and there are plans to ship them out of Mexico."

"Yes. This is true. If we can identify them as two missing citizens of the United States who were murdered here in Sonora, we will send them back to their family in Arizona."

Jones was amused to see the large doctor actually splutter.

"But Mexican law forbids this! A body must be buried for five years before it is disinterred, and then special permission must be granted in order to remove it from Mexican soil."

Jones thought that the doctor spoke with all the passion and emotion he must have used when he had taken the Hippocratic Oath.

"Believe me, Señor Doctor, I am aware of this, but due to the serious criminal matter in which Colonel Kosterlitsky is assisting the North American authorities, he felt that time was of the essence and contacted his friend Dr. Lovato directly." The lieutenant shrugged his shoulders.

"The colonel is in charge of this?" the doctor asked. "Yes, Señor Doctor, and I am sure that an honest error was made in your not being notified," the lieutenant explained.

"Yes. Yes. Of course." The doctor nervously stroked his thick mustache and stood. "No matter. Please give the colonel my compliments. I am sure he instructed Dr. Lovato to notify me. Well!" He drew himself up. "I will certainly have a few words with Dr. Lovato."

They exchanged a few pleasantries, and the lieutenant escorted the chief medical officer to the door. After the doctor left, the same nurse who had announced his arrival entered with a tray of coffee and a plate of pastries. She placed the tray on the desk and turned to leave.

"*Momentito*, señora." Holguín held up his hand. He introduced himself and Jones to her. "And your name?" he asked politely.

"Maria Elena." She smiled. "And not señora, but señorita."

Holguín's smile broadened at her declaration of being single. "Thank you for the coffee and pastries. *Muy amable!*"

She smiled at the lieutenant and gave Jones a shy look. Holguín's eyes followed her out of the room. He sighed and poured coffee for Jones and himself.

"Is there a problem with the bodies?" Jones had a frown on his face.

"No. No problem for us, Owen. The doctor has his rules and regulations, and he must enforce them just as I do mine, but we both know that this matter is more about his dignity as chief medical officer. Our meeting preserved that dignity by recognizing his authority, and he has fulfilled his duty by advising us of the laws and rules under his jurisdiction. There is no doubt that young Dr. Lovato will be reminded by the chief medical officer, in no uncertain terms, of these laws, regulations, and, most of all, his authority." He chuckled.

"But what about the laws concerning the bodies?" Jones sipped his coffee.

"Oh, why, we will ignore them, of course." Holguín waved his hand and laughed.

They sat in Dr. Lovato's office, drinking coffee and discussing the location and possible future plans of Mitchell and his gang, and after a while, Ashley came in through the back door and told them that the doctor had finished the exam.

SEVENTEEN

⬥

Holguín and Jones followed Ashley across a large mani-cured lawn to a white three-story building, through the doors, and down the stairs to the basement. The smell of disinfectant and the other familiar smells of a hospital did not quite mask the strong odor of a morgue. They entered a small but orderly room with a cement slab in the center over which Dr. Lovato stood. The remains of the two bodies lay before him. He looked up at Jones and Holguín.

"I can definitely tell you that they are female. I would estimate the larger one as being in her mid-forties and the smaller one eight to ten years old. The older one has a deep cut on the ante-rior face of cervical vertebra number three, which would be con-sistent with a very violent cutting or hacking blow through—" He caught himself and explained, "What I mean is that whoever did this cut through her trachea and the entire structure of her neck. With just a bit more force, her head would have been severed."

The doctor moved his hand over to the smaller pile of bones. "This little one's death appears to have been caused by severe trauma to the brain and internal organs, judging by the damage to the skull and ribcage. It is as if she fell from a great height and landed square on her face and chest. Her skull and ribcage ..." he pointed with his finger and continued, "were crushed. There is no doubt that she died instantly."

Dr. Lovato watched as Jones nodded grimly. When there were no questions, he said, "There is something else." He pointed to several areas of what had been the girl's body. "Here on the radius and ulna and again on the humerus on the left side. And here on the metacarpals and phalanges of both hands, notice these healed fractures." He pointed to small bumps that were lighter in color than the surrounding bone. "And again, here on the right tibia, there is another one. I think there may have been at least one healed fracture above the supraorbital notch of the skull, but there is too much recent damage to say for certain."

Jones looked at the doctor with a tortured look of understanding. "Could they have been caused by a fall from a horse or some type of playground accident?"

"Possibly, but I doubt it. These injuries have all healed at different times over a period of five or six years. Also, the injuries to the arms and hands are parts of the body that are often used in a defensive motion." He demonstrated by holding up his arms and ducking his head. "No, Mr. Jones. In my opinion, this child suffered, over a period of years, some serious physical abuse."

Jones said nothing. He just looked down at the little pile of bones. He could feel the hate rising in him and fought against it as he thought of the gruff old rancher MacDuff. He asked the doctor, "Would these injuries have to be treated by a doctor?"

"It is interesting that you ask, because I find that two of the more acute fractures appear to have been set by someone with medical experience. I am almost certain a doctor attended these injuries. There is something else. Actually, it was your partner here who pointed it out to me. After careful examination of the hip structure of the older one, we can say with a fair degree of certainty that she had never experienced childbirth. We naturally assumed that this was mother and daughter, but now I don't think so." Dr. Lovato recognized the internal struggle Jones was trying to cover up. "I will make a written report and give you a copy. I have also arranged for some coffins to transport the remains back to Arizona. Is there anything else I can do to help?"

"No. Thank you for all you have done. I can certainly use your report. It will be very important in any prosecution of the men who committed this crime." Jones's voice was as tight as the expression on his face. It was like that on the very few occasions in his life when he told a bald-faced lie. There would be no trial. He would kill the men who had done this. He would hunt every one of them down, even those who had stood by and done nothing but watch it happen in that peaceful little glade by the river. He would hunt them all down. Badge or no badge. In Mexico or back in the States, it did not matter. He would kill every last one of them. It was the promise he had made back at the river, and he would carry this promise until it was done. No one else shared the promise. It was his alone. And after it was over, he would deal with Old Man MacDuff.

After Sergeant Montaño and his scouting party, who were now dressed in civilian clothes, rode off to the east, the rest of the *rurales* and the two rangers rode west to Magdalena to meet with the colonel and plan for the tracking down of Mitchell and his gang in the Sierras. They arrived at the colonel's late that night with just enough time for a decent meal and a good night's rest.

EIGHTEEN

ones sat next to Holguín in the second row of chairs set up in a large room at the colonel's hacienda. He was freshly shaved and wore his newly purchased jacket over a clean white shirt and tie. He did not know what to expect at a music recital, having never been to one, but he was prepared to put up with whatever the afternoon in the cool room offered. When the colonel had extended the invitation at breakfast, he had spoken to them as if Jones and Ashley routinely attended music recitals. It was as casual as being invited to a Sunday poker game in the bunkhouse. Jones was reluctant but reminded himself that he was a representative of Captain Wheeler and the rangers. As soon as they had accepted, Jones had escaped to the stables to brush down his horse even though the stable boy had already seen to it.

So he sat, dressed like everyone else in the room, as if for church. He hoped that the ordeal would not be as tedious as a brimstone-and-hellfire preaching but was resigned to endure the children and their music as best he could. Thoughts of the Mitchell gang began to run through his mind, but he found it difficult to concentrate on them as he watched the young children under the serious scrutiny of their parents set up various stringed instruments, music stands, and sheet music. The small raised stage was dominated by a very large piano. It was black, and the afternoon light reflected off the expensive looking coat of lacquer. The piano was a long and graceful instrument, so unlike the upright pianos that were commonplace in the saloons of Arizona. He sighed to himself and studied the one-page program, realizing that he did not recognize the title of one single song. A trickle of sweat ran down his back as he thought of the formal dinner he was to attend after the recital. He made a conscious effort to ignore the sweat and steeled himself to spend the rest of the afternoon and evening in his stiff collar and tie.

As he sat there wishing he had bought a larger collar, the side door to the room opened, and a young girl carrying a violin case was ushered into the room by the most beautiful woman Jones had ever seen. The girl appeared to be seven or eight years old with light brown hair and freckles, and she strongly resembled the woman behind her. The woman closed the door behind her and looked at Jones, smiled, and waved at him. Before his bewildered mind could grasp what had just happened, he noticed Holguín raise his hand and discreetly wave at the woman and child.

"My cousin and her daughter," Holguín whispered to Jones as if they were in church.

Jones could not take his eyes off the woman. Her beauty held his attention, but he was also struck by her bearing. She was not as reserved and did not hold herself with the same formality as other women in the room, but she seemed both confident and serene and brought a natural calm to the group of young musicians who surrounded her as soon as she stepped onto the stage. Evidently, she was the director of the recital. He watched as she quickly organized the children and helped them set up their instruments and sheet music. She then gave a formal introduction of the children and the pieces of music each would play. Her voice had a natural authority, and she obviously would be comfortable in any setting. Suddenly, the prospect of a long-suffering afternoon faded from Jones's mind. Holguín was amused to see Jones relax and even smile.

For the next hour, Jones watched as the woman directed the young musicians. When a particularly complex piece required more skill at the piano than the youngsters possessed, she would take her place at the keyboard and provide an understated accompaniment to the string quartet. Jones was not sure whether it was the music or the woman or a combination of both, but he was very much at peace. His immediate reaction was one of caution, but he ignored all the inner warnings and slowly dropped his guard as he became captivated by the delicate, pure elegance of the music.

After the recital, while the children gathered around a table covered with goblets of ice cream, Holguín introduced Jones to the woman. "Señora Catalina Luisa Gallegos de San Martín," she said as she reached out and shook his hand. "And that little one with a mouth full of ice cream is my daughter, María Cristina." Her eyes held him captive, and Jones realized that he was holding on to her hand longer than would seem proper in this setting. He could not remember ever having so many words come to the tip of his tongue at the same time but only managed to tell her how much he enjoyed the music.

"How very kind of you to attend, Mr. Jones. I hope you were not too disappointed by our interpretations of the great composers." She laughed. And when she laughed, he felt like they were the only two people in the room.

"I enjoyed it very much!" He silently cursed for repeating himself.

"Well then, Mr. Jones, perhaps you will return for more." She looked directly into his eyes and smiled.

Parents and children came up to her in a constant stream, congratulating her and engaging in brief small talk. He excused himself, intending to leave her to her friends and admirers, but she reached out and caught his sleeve.

"No, Mr. Jones. Stay. I have not had the occasion to speak with someone from Arizona in a long while." She noticed him look around the room and sensed his concern. She spoke to him in a soft voice. "If you are looking for my *marido*, you must know that I have none. I am a widow."

Later as they walked out in the shade of a long porch on the courtyard, they talked of current events in the States, and he learned that her father had business interests there and that twice a year, she brought her daughter to Phoenix for the symphony as well as the performances of traveling ballet troupes. She was curious about his life and experiences, but she asked her questions in a subtle and understated manner. She noticed that he answered her questions without elaboration and that his manner was not evasive, but rather indifferent, as if his past held little interest for him.

Jones found Catalina to be knowledgeable about the cattle business. She spoke in some depth about all aspects of ranch life. She told him that she and her husband had had a large operation south of Magdalena, and had been in the process of importing bulls from Texas for an experiment in crossbreeding when her husband had been struck and killed by lightning while out gathering cattle.

"Poor Ernesto! It killed him and his favorite stallion. But I believe he was happy when he died because he was where he wanted to be and was doing what he loved."

"Do you miss him?" Jones wanted to bring this conversation to an end.

She looked at Jones and did not say anything for a moment. Her eyes were full of questions.

"I do miss him, but not as much as before. After almost a year, it serves no purpose. It may sound cold, but it is the truth."

In the silence that followed, they noticed that they were alone in the courtyard.

"It would be wonderful to stay and enjoy the peace and quiet with you, Mr. Jones, but I must see to María Cristina and prepare for tonight. You will be there, won't you?"

Wild horses couldn't pull me away, he thought, but he told her matter-of-factly, "Yes, I will," and opened the door for her.

"Until then, Mr. Jones." She smiled and went back inside.

Jones walked out onto the large courtyard, his mind filled with the sound of her voice. From a distance, he heard Holguín call out to him. He was embarrassed to realize that he was walking off in the wrong direction. Get hold of yourself, he thought, and he turned and walked over to Holguín.

NINETEEN

———◆———

Spence lounged on the settee in his hotel suite and puffed on a cigar as he concentrated on his plans for the train robbery. At first, he considered making his move above the junction town of Benjamin Hill, but that would bring the action too close to Magdalena and the large force of *rurales* stationed there. He then considered the option of boarding the train at Hermosillo and taking his action somewhere in the vicinity of Carbo, where the road led east through a largely unpopulated area that would ensure easy traveling and a quicker route back to the Sierras. This option had the advantage of placing greater distance between the gang and any pursuit by either the *rurales* or the army. After exploring several other options, he decided that the plan to board at Hermosillo made the most sense. Now the only problem was to get Mitchell and his gang to be prepared to move from their camp in the mountains to Hermosillo within the next four or five days. Earlier in the week, he had sent word to Mitchell to meet him near a small village in the foothills east of La Plata and had made plans to travel there by train tomorrow.

"John, come back to bed." Her full lips were set in a fake pout as she sat propped against a bunch of pillows, holding a glass of champagne.

Spence sighed and put his cigar in an ashtray. He had not noticed the annoying demand in her voice before. She required a lot of his attention, and he was beginning to wonder if he had made a mistake. Her long, dark hair fell over her shoulders onto the pillows. She wore only the pearl choker her husband had bought for her in the capital and smiled that same incredible smile he had first seen on the train. He ran his fingers over the polished pearls, noticing that their hard brilliance formed a perfect contrast to her soft skin. Perhaps I didn't make a mistake after all, he thought.

Later that day he sat on the ground in a small copse of trees uphill from the village and listened to a couple of mountain jays fuss at each other in the shadows of the undergrowth. The rented mule grazed next to the footpath leading back to the village, and he felt the chill of a light breeze slipping down from the mountains. He had no expectation that Mitchell would arrive on time, so he relaxed and watched the late-afternoon sun go behind some clouds in the west.

In a little while, two of Mitchell's men, one behind and one in front of him, approached cautiously with drawn pistols. They came quietly to within fifteen feet, stopped, and waited, and then one of them gave a soft whistle. Within a minute, Mitchell sat on the ground across from him without a word, studying Spence's rough clothing and high, laced engineer boots, but his face remained expressionless and he sat, waiting for Spence to speak.

Spence knew better than to waste his time with any greetings or small talk, so he immediately began explaining the robbery scheme and described how the payroll was shipped from Hermosillo to the mine headquarters in Cananea. Very slowly and deliberately, he went over the details of the security of the shipment on the train. Then he went over it again. He described where McLeod would be on the train and what he would be wearing and how they were to use McLeod to gain access to the express car and the payroll. He then laid out the escape route, stressing the need for the men to head east on two different routes to split any pursuit. Then, after picking out several rendezvous points and fallback locations, Spence sat back and asked Mitchell if he had any questions.

"Where you gonna be?" The man's eyes were flat as he looked at Spence.

"I will meet you at the first rendezvous point. You can give me my share, and we'll split up until next time." Spence grinned. He had always been careful in what he said to Mitchell. The man was a volcano about to erupt, and Spence handled him with a delicate balance of respect and strength. Not too much of either, because Mitchell habitually rebelled against strong instructions and would pounce in an instant on anyone who appeared weak. Spence believed that he had Mitchell's confidence, if not his full trust, because they had both made a lot of money together.

"This bookkeeper, how much is his share?" Mitchell asked.

Spence gave him the figure and said he would collect McLeod's share at the rendezvous and deliver it to him later.

"How much of the money is in pesos?" Mitchell asked.

"I don't know exactly, probably five or six thousand. You can have all the pesos and coin. All I want is my share in dollars."

Mitchell sat silently, as if he were digesting the entire plan, and then abruptly stood.

"OK. We will be on the train just like you say." He turned and walked back up the hill. After he disappeared into the shadows, his two men followed and Spence was once again alone.

Spence sat there a while, slightly concerned as he always was when dealing with this man. There was no one better in a situation that required force or threat of violence. Mitchell was fearless and ruthless, and that was always the problem. Sometimes Mitchell could not control his violence, and then all hell was unleashed. But Spence had no choice. He would have to depend on him because Mitchell was a very important part of the plan.

Spence walked down the path and grabbed the reins of the mule and led him back up the hill. He would camp out here and head back to La Plata in the morning in time for the morning train to Hermosillo.

TWENTY

---✦---

J ones was flustered. The boiled collar cut into the freshly shaved skin under his jaw, and his Adam's apple pushed against the knot of his tie. The cool of the embroidered tablecloth brushed his knuckles as he sat stiffly with his hands folded on his lap. The confusing array of china and silver-plated knives, forks, and spoons set before him added to his nervous state, and he hoped his confusion was not being observed by the others at the table in the colonel's huge dining room. He had counted twenty-five people at the table, and the civilian men were dressed in fine suits the like of which Jones had rarely seen in the States. The colonel's officers wore the silver-trimmed gray uniforms with white shirts and black ties, and the women were wrapped in the finest silk dresses with all kinds of ruffles, frills, and lace that enhanced their confident beauty and graceful manners. He was glad his scuffed boots and shabby wool trousers were out of sight beneath the table.

Adding to his unease was the fact that directly across the table from him, sitting next to Ashley, was Catalina Luisa Gallegos de San Martín. When he managed to look up from his study of the silverware, confused about the purpose of each piece, their eyes would meet and she would smile at him. His heartbeat would increase; he would smile back and immediately go back to studying the silverware. You idiot, he thought, you can't go on like this all night. He decided to watch Ashley closely and follow his lead in the use of the various pieces.

Ashley was completely at ease. His suit was every bit as fine as any in the room, and he talked and laughed confidently with Catalina. The colonel clinked a knife against his wine goblet, and all eyes turned to the head of the table as he offered a toast to the president and the republic. Jones sipped politely from his wine glass and hoped his face did not betray his dislike for the taste of the wine; he truly wondered why people drank this stuff. There were many toasts to follow, and after the second glass of wine Jones grudgingly admitted to himself that it wasn't that bad. In fact, it went well with the numerous courses of the meal. He began to relax sometime between the soup and fish course and joined in the conversations around him. The talk flowed freely between Spanish and English, and his dining companions were polite about his improper Spanish grammar and incorrect use of the tenses. He noticed that Ashley and Catalina were speaking in yet another language he recognized, but it sounded very different from the New Orleans French he had heard in his youth.

After the meal, the women retired to another room, and as the brandy and cigars were brought, Jones excused himself and stepped out into the courtyard. He stood there, grateful for the slight breeze and the stars dancing above the hills in the east, and he felt the closeness of the dining room begin to sift away, and even the stiffness of his collar did not seem so harsh. The flare of a match behind him snapped him out of his thoughts, and he quickly turned in a half crouch.

"Hello, Mr. Jones." Catalina stood, calmly puffing on a thin brown cigarillo. "I am glad you are not wearing a gun. It might have shortened our conversation." She smoked and watched him. He could see her eyes in the half light, a mischievous glint of green.

He relaxed and she walked up next to him.

"Your colleague, Ashley, has told me stories about you. I wanted to see for myself if you are as interesting as he made you sound." She laughed. "And if you think me forward for doing so, you are correct. I despise any politeness that masks pretense and cannot abide words that hide hypocrisy, and I especially do not like timid people."

Jones laughed and shook his head. "Señora de San Martín, I could never say it as pretty as you just did, but those are my feelings exactly."

"I am glad we are already in agreement, but one more thing, Mr. Jones." She walked over and stood next to him. "A widow in Mexico must wear her widowhood like a heavy black shawl for all to see. We widows are expected to carry our grief with us at all times and only exchange sadness with others. You should know that I am sick to death of sadness and of being the *viuda* de San Martín." She said all this in a conversational tone with no bitterness or rancor. "So please, call me Catalina, and I will call you Owen."

Jones tried to keep his breathing normal. In the space of an afternoon and evening, this woman had made him struggle with thoughts and feelings that confused him. Since he had first seen her come into the music room, he could hardly think of anything else. He had been impatient to get started after the killers, wherever they were, but now all he wanted was to be with this woman. He thought of the other women he had been with and tried to remember how he had felt when he had met them. Enchantment? Curiosity? Desire? Happiness? Some of each maybe, but not all, and certainly not all of it in one woman.

"I would like that very much, Catalina."

They stood next to each other, the noise of the dinner party and the low murmur of conversation of other people in the courtyard behind them. After a while, Catalina moved away from him and walked over to a large group of rose bushes trellised against an adobe wall. She spoke to him over her shoulder. "I am very curious, Owen. How is it you manage to face the uncertainty of it all?" She stood with her back to him, admiring the roses.

"Uncertainty?" He had not moved.

"What I mean is ..." She turned and seemed surprised that he still stood where she had left him. She smiled to herself and walked over to him. "It seems to me that there is a great deal of uncertainty in your work. I mean when you confront these desperados that you hunt down. There must be an even chance that you may be hurt or killed in these instances. So I was curious as to how you dealt with the unknown on each occasion."

Jones could not think of a reply because he realized he did not fully understand her question. Uncertainty? What did she mean by that? At times, he had considered the odds of being killed or injured, but the tone of her question put a whole new twist on the possibility of it happening.

Catalina saw the puzzled look on Jones's face and realized she had confused him and made him uncomfortable. She immediately regretted her words and moved closer to him and took his hand. "I will tell you, Owen, if you promise to forgive me for my silly question, I promise never to ask another. What I really wanted to ask you is this: Can you find time to visit my ranch and share your opinions of the crossbreeding project with the shorthorns?"

"I didn't think it was a silly question, it's just ..."

"The ranch, Owen. Will you visit?" She squeezed his hand.

"Yes. Sure. We have no plans for tomorrow. Is it far?"

"An easy one-hour ride, Nicolás can give you directions. Tomorrow, then?" Still holding his hand, she pulled him back into the shadowed light of the tiled courtyard.

"Yes, tomorrow." Jones felt his heart beat faster. They strolled around the courtyard, and he could not remember a more perfect evening.

TWENTY-ONE

⸻◆⸻

The Hotel Cuahtemoc had been built with American money for Americans when President Porfirio Díaz began his push to attract foreign investment into Mexico. In the years since, modern, more opulent hotels had been built closer to the center of town, and the Cuahtemoc sat in the shadows of the old Hermosillo business district. The hotel still did a steady business, but her clientele were the new businessmen trying to carve out a piece of the fortune to be had in northern Mexico or those who were no longer prospering. Although the hotel could not hide her age or the frailties of old engineering, her staff maintained the same high quality and solid dignity of the days when she had been known as the Queen of Sonora.

Spence walked through the lobby, past the old-fashioned wooden desks and overstuffed chairs in the guest registration area, past the creaky, old-fashioned lift, and up the wide marble staircase to the ambassador's suite on the second floor. Without knocking, he opened the two carved oak doors and entered to find his two colleagues seated on the brocade divans in the sitting room. The younger of the two stood, nodded to him, then went over to lock the door behind him. The older man, who wore a perpetual expression of apology, remained seated. Spence walked over and shook the old man's hand.

"How are you, Daniel?" Spence asked with genuine concern. This old counterfeiter was the closest thing to a father that Spence had in his life.

"Fine, thank you." The old man sat very formally and stiffly on the divan. There was a large steamer trunk on the floor in front of him.

Spence glanced at the trunk and sat in a chair facing both men. "I won't waste any time because we don't have much of it," he told them. "I need Sir James"—he nodded to the younger man and continued—"for another week or so. And Daniel, all I need from you is the paper I mentioned on the telephone."

The old man nodded and put his hand on the trunk. "I brought all the notes that were left, both dollars and pounds sterling. I took down the press, broke the plates, and moved everything out of the shop. I won't be going back."

The younger man came over and laid the trunk on its side. Daniel handed him the key and watched as the young man opened the trunk and began pulling open the drawers inside. The young man stacked bundles of paper money on the floor next to the trunk. Spence had always admired the skill of the old man because he was an unusual talent in the counterfeiting business. He was both an expert engraver and printer and had worked with Benjamin Boyd, the greatest counterfeiter of his time. Daniel was an artist with the soul of an engineer, as meticulous in the preparation of the steel plates as he was in the selection of inks and paper. But Spence had concerns about the old man's health. During the past several years, when he had had occasion to deal with him, Spence had noticed the thicker eyeglasses and the more pronounced tremors in Daniel's left hand.

"The dollars are excellent," the old man pronounced, pointing to a separate pile of notes, "but, except for about five thousand, the pound sterling notes are not. I was unable to secure the proper steel for the plates. It was too soft, but I ran off a batch anyway." He nodded to the younger man, who picked up a bundle of pound notes and handed them to Spence, who took his time carefully examining several notes.

"You have me, Daniel. They look fine to me."

"Look at the royal seal." Daniel pointed.

Spence looked very carefully and, after a few moments, held up a ten-pound note and laughed. "Daniel, isn't the unicorn supposed to have a horn?" He laughed again.

The old man's apologetic look was more pronounced. "Yes, and I should have destroyed the notes when I broke up the plates, but I didn't. There is a total of twenty-five thousand pounds, and if you can use them, take them with my best wishes. I know you won't be using a pusher, so I have no fear of them being circulated. They could be used for flash if you sandwich them between the good notes, but I wouldn't go any farther than that."

Spence held the stack of notes, studying them. "I might just have a use for them after all. Now let's see the American notes."

They spent the next hour counting out the notes and then settled on their standard fee. Spence pulled a stack of bills from a large wallet, counted them out, and handed them to Daniel.

The old man took the money and looked over at the stack of counterfeit notes as if reluctant to part with them. He sighed and then slowly stood up. "As always, I want to wish you the best of luck in your new business venture."

"Where are you off to, Daniel?" Spence stood and came over to shake his hand.

"I will catch the two o'clock train to Guaymas, where I have booked passage on a ship out of Mexico. You can reach me through the usual arrangements in San Francisco." He nodded formally. "Good evening, gentlemen."

Spence walked over to open the door. "Take care, Daniel." Spence felt a genuine sadness, as if it might be the last time he would see the old man. He watched as Daniel walked slowly down the corridor. Spence then locked the door and went back into the sitting room.

"And now, Sir James, here is the plan."

TWENTY-TWO

D el Castillo studied Sir James from behind his desk. The Englishman sat with his injured leg straight out in front of him, apparently at ease in the leather-covered straight-back chair. The lawyer had dealt with Englishmen in the past, and he held them in contempt. They were poor business-men, demanding when they should be flexible, and completely indifferent to the finer points of negotiation. And this one with his eye patch and cane reminded him of the damned Spaniards in that they seemed more interested in titles and military medals than success in business.

"Your concerns about the correct structure of the corporate entity you wish to establish are well founded. I can assure you that my colleagues and I will arrange for the creation of your corporation and obtain for you all the necessary permits, li-censes, and other legal documents." Del Castillo leaned back in his chair.

"So good to hear that. I am in rather a hurry to form the com-pany since I have an opportunity to purchase several ships at a very attractive price, and, well, there are the berthing rights and all that, you see." The Englishman waved his hand.

Del Castillo sensed his own opportunity. "We can move quickly, but I must advise you that it is always more expensive to expedite business dealings in the republic."

"No matter, I am prepared to deal with that." Again, he waved his hand dismissively.

Excellent, thought del Castillo; the fees have just doubled. "We can start this morning. I will proceed along the lines you have laid out in your business proposal." He put his hand on a small stack of paper on his desk. "And the documents will be ready for your signature by late afternoon tomorrow."

"Thank you." Sir James seemed distracted.

"I will need the name of your bank for the corporate records," del Castillo said.

"Yes, well ..." The Englishman frowned and cleared his throat. "I have always handled my financial affairs in a most discreet manner, and my question to you is, simply, shall I expect to continue to do so in this venture?"

The lawyer suppressed a chuckle at the opportunity for even more control of the Englishman's money he had just been given. He made a steeple of his fingers and placed them under his chin. "Well, Sir James, the scrutiny of our banking system by the officials in the capital is very strenuous, to say the least. However," he said, holding up one hand in confidence, "I assure you that I can guarantee complete privacy in how the corporation's financial operations are run. All I ask is that you keep me advised of any major expenditures or movement of funds so I can be prepared to deal with any, shall we say, difficulty caused by our bureaucracy."

"Yes, yes, of course. Tomorrow morning, I expect delivery of a considerable sum in pounds sterling. Naturally, an appropriate amount will be deposited to establish a banking account; however, I wish to keep the bulk of it out of the public eye, so to speak. You see, my plans require substantial funds, very liquid in nature, which can flow freely and quickly with the minimum of paperwork."

"Of course, Sir James. I have experience in such matters, and I can assure you complete security and quick access. I recommend the Banco del Mar the bank of record for purposes of the corporation. It is the most prestigious bank in the north, and I am on good terms with its board of directors."

They discussed a few more details and made arrangements for the next day's meeting and the processing of Sir James's funds. The Englishman stood and del Castillo escorted him to the door, then watched from his window as he limped down the street, a polished oak cane in his left hand.

Two days after signing the corporate papers and turning twenty-five thousand pounds sterling over to del Castillo, Sir James returned to the lawyer's office.

"I'm afraid I will require cash much sooner than I had anticipated." He had a chagrined look on his face.

"Of course, Sir James, and how much will you require?" del Castillo turned to the large safe in the corner of his office. "Twenty thousand in pounds sterling. My sources have learned of an unannounced distress sale involving several ships ..." The Englishman broke off as he watched del Castillo return from the safe.

"That is indeed wonderful news." The lawyer began placing stacks of Mexican pesos on his desk.

"But the pounds sterling?" Sir James was flustered.

"Oh, Sir James, you will find it much easier to deal in pesos here in the republic!" He kept bringing pesos from the safe to his desk.

"But the pound sterling is highly favored here in Mexico!" Sir James sputtered.

"Sir James, please!" del Castillo stood behind his desk. "I am well aware of that and fully intend to credit the difference to your account. After all, this is 'off the books,' as the North Americans say, and I have a separate ledger to account for the difference. We can go over the numbers whenever you like in order to ensure your complete satisfaction. In fact, let me get the numbers now."

"No, no. That will not be necessary today. I am in a bit of rush, you see." Sir James stood up.

Del Castillo smiled at the Englishman. He had counted on his inattention to the details of business. And now, he thought, your pound notes are in my account enjoying a very handsome rate of interest. He knew Sir James would never have the desire or perhaps even the ability to decipher the figures of international currency transactions in the numerous ledgers he had established. It was almost too easy.

TWENTY-THREE

S alvador was leading his father's five goats up into the hills
when he saw the men ride out of the east onto the main
street of his village. He stopped and watched them. The
small village was well off the beaten path, and the only
visitors were the *rurales* and occasionally some mining engineers
or hunting parties of North Americans passing through. The village had always been isolated. The only regular contact with out-
siders had occurred in the old days, when the Apaches had
hidden in the Sierras. Salvador had grown up listening to his father's stories of the old days when the Apaches would come in
from their camps for aguardiente and supplies. The older people
had been afraid of the Apaches but had managed to get along
with them even though there were occasional conflicts. The village chief, Don Alfonso, and Salvador's father had walked many
miles to the Indian camp to meet with their chief and make arrangements for peaceful exchanges of goods between the Apaches
and the villagers. These arrangements had confirmed in the villagers' minds their wisdom in choosing Don Alfonso as their
chief. The Apaches had left the Sierras many years ago, but from
time to time, bandidos would come to the mountains and hide

from the authorities. The *rurales* or soldiers would either capture or kill them, and as a result, the village had enjoyed long years of relative peace.

These men that Salvador now watched had been to the village for supplies before, and although they drank a lot, they had not caused trouble. They were hard-looking men, and there were some gringos among them, their Texas-style hats standing out among the larger Mexican sombreros. Salvador counted two gringos among the twelve riders. He wanted to stay and watch them, but the goats were wandering away, and he ran after them.

Don Alfonso watched the riders as they gathered in front of the village store. He knew they would want the regular staples of beans and corn and tinned goods and they would probably exhaust the storekeeper's supply of liquor. The leader of the riders went into the store with several of his companions. The others lounged in front of the store, and several wandered down to sit in the shade of the bandstand in the small plaza. Don Alfonso had seen these men before when they had drifted through the district in the spring. He had heard that they had been seen as far east as Casas Grandes, but they had returned to the village several weeks ago, so he had sent word to the colonel that they were back. He and Hilario, the storekeeper, had talked about the gang and had hoped they would not return, but now they were back.

"*Malditos!*" he said to himself. He had known bad ones like these in the old days. He only hoped that they would remain peaceful while they were here getting supplies. Sometimes even the worst of men, when they found themselves taking part in the normalcy of everyday life such as buying supplies, tended to accept being part of their civilized surroundings and could act peacefully. Still, he could not remember seeing men that caused him greater concern.

One of the men came out of Hilario's store with a bottle of aguardiente, gave it to one of the gringos, and then went back inside.

"Oh, God! Please give us your help and send these men on their way," Don Alfonso prayed. He slipped into his house and watched them from the window. The men passed the bottle around. Within a few minutes, it was empty. The group from the plaza came hurrying back when they saw the bottle but shared only in the few remaining sips. One of them went inside the store and returned with two full bottles, which the men immediately began consuming. All hope for a peaceful day left Don Alfonso when the men finished the second bottle, threw both empties into the street, and began shooting at them with their pistols.

The shooting brought the leader out of the store with his gun in his hand, and when he saw what was happening, he laughed and grabbed the remaining bottle from the gringo and took several big gulps. He handed back the bottle and went inside. After a while, the men began bringing supplies out of the store and loading them on their horses. Now, Don Alfonso thought, we will be rid of these *malditos*, but his relief turned to horror when he saw the children slowly make their way up the street from the plaza, curious about the strangers and their laughter and gunplay.

Hilario's daughter, Eliselma, ran after the children, scolding them and telling them to come back. The girl was tall for her fourteen years, and she was in charge of taking the children to catechism classes taught by the nuns at the church. Eliselma's frantic efforts paid off, and the children hurried back toward the plaza. Don Alfonso noticed the evil-looking gringo stare at Eliselma and then step out onto the street. The gringo covered the short distance to the plaza very quickly. Don Alfonso ran out the back door of his house and down the alleyway to the plaza, but when he got there, the gringo already had the girl by the arm and was forcing her to go with him back to the store. Don Alfonso gathered the other children and pushed them in the direction of the nuns, who were coming out of the church. He then turned and walked back up the street to Hilario's store. The men watched him approach with no real concern; they were laughing at the gringo, who was having a hard time controlling the young girl.

Don Alfonso stopped in front of the men just as their leader came out of the store. A dark cloud of despair passed over Don Alfonso as he saw the gleam in the bandit chief's eye when he looked at Eliselma.

The village chief spoke loudly with all the authority he possessed. "Leave the girl alone!" he ordered.

The gringo turned and looked at him as if he was not sure he understood. The leader walked over and grabbed the girl.

The look in the leader's eye frightened Don Alfonso more than all of these men with all their guns. "For the sake of God! Do not molest this little one!" he demanded again.

"She doesn't look that little to me, old man." The leader drew his pistol and pointed it at Don Alfonso. "Go away! Or I will send you to your god."

Don Alfonso stood his ground. "You call yourselves men?" He was about to say more when the leader cocked his pistol and pulled the trigger. The bullet hit the ground inches away from Don Alfonso's feet, and he forced himself not to flinch. The bandit fired two more shots at the old man's feet. Even though he wanted to, the bandit could not kill the unarmed old man like this. The old fool did not even carry a machete. The men were laughing and passing the bottle. The bandit pushed the girl back to the gringo and walked over to the old man, who stood there glaring at him. He swung his pistol and hit the old man on the head. Don Alfonso swayed but remained on his feet. The bandit hit him in the stomach with his fist, and when Don Alfonso doubled over, the bandit hit him on the head with his pistol again. The old man fell to the ground. The bandit then kicked him in the ribs.

"Next time, you'll listen to me, you old bastard!" He turned and walked back to his men, who were grinning at him. He grabbed the girl from the gringo and handed her to one of the other men. "Panchito! Bring her along, and keep Zeke away from her." He walked to his horse and pulled himself up into the saddle.

Suddenly, Hilario burst out of the store, carrying an old muzzle-loading rifle. The bandit chief looked at him with amusement. Now this one, he thought, is armed. He drew his pistol and fired two rounds into Hilario, who crumpled and fell into the open doorway of his store. The leader holstered his pistol, dismounted, and walked back into the store, stepping over Hilario's body. In a moment, he came back out of the store, holding three more bottles of liquor and a handful of cash. The men cheered and began laughing. He handed the bottles to one of the men, mounted his horse, and led his men down the street. Eliselma was slung like a sack of flour over Panchito's saddle. The man held her firmly as she struggled and screamed as they rode east out of the village.

Several of the villagers gathered around Don Alfonso and helped him to his feet before leading him over to one of the benches in the plaza.

"Bring Salvador! Quickly!" he instructed.

His wife dabbed at the gash on his forehead with a piece of cloth soaked in aguardiente as the others looked on. After a while, Salvador came running up the street to the plaza.

"Salvador! Take the mule and get word to the colonel. Tell him they have killed Hilario and they have taken Eliselma! Quickly!"

TWENTY-FOUR

ngel lay on his back in a bed of pine needles near a large tree and looked up at the clear mountain sky. The tree swayed in a small breeze and then split in two, swayed in the opposite direction and then grew back together into one tree again. It had been doing this for the past several hours as he lay there drinking aguardiente. The alcohol blurred the colors of the sky and tree branches, and they moved together in ever-growing circles. The aguardiente kept him warm in the breeze, and he could feel a slight numbness begin in his limbs and move slowly to his face. It was peaceful here and he thought pleasant thoughts and was happy in the quiet of his hiding place.

But each time the girl's screams echoed up the barranca from the camp below, he brought the bottle to his mouth and drank deeply. He did not think he could go far enough up the mountain to escape her screams. After a while, the peaceful thoughts he had been enjoying under his tree began to slowly leave him. For most of his life he had never thought very highly of himself. He was lazy, he was a thief, and he had killed people. His family called him *sinverguenza*, shameless, and he agreed, but he knew, deep in his core, he could never do the disgraceful things that some of his compadres were doing to the *pobrecita* down in the camp, or what they had done to the gringas at the river. Did they not have mothers or sisters? He took a long drink from the bottle.

At times he had thought about leaving the gang, but there was always food and plenty of drink. He was weak and would not survive long on his own, so he always stayed. Yes, he thought, he always stayed. He took another drink, and he felt the numbness begin to take hold, and the girl's screams weakened and became less bothersome to him. The tree and sky began turning in tighter circles. He closed his eyes to make it stop, but his body began to spin, and as he lay there spinning with the trees and the sky, he thought he heard his name being called. "Ángel! Ángel!" His name came echoing up the canyon. He was very tired and closed his eyes, but the spinning only got worse.

When he awoke, he saw that the bottle had tipped over and the remaining liquor had poured out and soaked into the pine needles. The light of day had started to fade, and it was very quiet. He listened for noise from the camp below but could hear nothing. He got up slowly, but his head hurt so badly that he lay back down. He waited a while and then got up and began to make his way down to the camp. His head felt like it was going to split open.

He found the camp deserted and walked over to the hut to ask where everyone had gone, but he found no one there. He walked in a big circle around the camp and realized that they had left him. He went back to the hut and found that it was still stocked with food and supplies, so he knew they would return. They would never leave everything behind if they were moving on. He tried to think some more, but his head hurt him too much. He sat down at the large table and found two full bottles of aguardiente. Well, he thought, I will have a pleasant wait for my compadres.

TWENTY-FIVE

············◆············

C atalina Luisa Gallegos de San Martín could ride as well as any man Jones had ever ridden with. She sat her horse as if born to the saddle. She wore English riding pants and high-topped polished boots, and from the way she handled her mount, it was apparent that she had never in her life even considered riding sidesaddle. She rode in the Mexican style, legs and back straight but not stiff, and even at a full gallop, she never leaned forward in the saddle. Her hair was tied at the nape of her neck with a black ribbon, and she wore a black, flat-brimmed Spanish hat. Jones's heart ached at the natural beauty of horse and rider. He could have watched her ride all day.

They had ridden out from her hacienda in the late morning to inspect a herd of mixed-breed shorthorns that was pastured in the eastern hills. They stopped at a gate that led to a fine pasture and watched the cattle graze in the midday sun. Jones had never seen this particular shorthorn mix but was impressed by the stoutness of their fore- and hindquarters. He and Catalina had discussed the research and methods of crossbreeding that Catalina and her late husband used, and Jones had learned that she was very knowledgeable about the bloodlines of the bulls and familiar with the latest studies in genetics. He had asked her questions about the qualities of black gramma versus drop-seed grass and the availability of water in this part of Mexico. They talked about this and other matters related to ranching as they rode back to the hacienda, but after a while, their conversation slowed as the subject of cattle was exhausted.

Catalina was still curious about details of his life, but when she asked him questions, he responded with short, shy answers. She was convinced that he was not ashamed or intentionally tried to hide facts but rather that he was not one who reflected much on his past. It would take patience on her part, she thought, but she was willing to invest it because she was convinced he was worth the effort.

They stopped on a knoll under a small stand of trees to eat a snack of cheese and fruit. Off to the east, they could see large white clouds form over the higher peaks of the Sierras. They were silent for a long time, as if giving each other a rest. She spoke first.

"Every time I see the Sierras, I think about how much I will miss them."

"You're thinking of leaving?" Jones was surprised.

"No, Owen. I am leaving."

"But why?"

"After Ernesto was killed, I thought about staying on and continuing Ernesto's work, but it did not make much sense. The possibilities for a widow here are not what I want for myself and María Cristina. I believe it is time to move on. And then there is Ernesto's family. Several months after his death, they began asking questions about my plans for the ranch even though my father put up most of the capital for its purchase."

"They didn't think a woman could run it?" he asked.

"No! That is not it!" Her eyes flashed at him. "They know me better than that! Ernesto was the oldest son, and his younger brother wants to annex this ranch to his. Anyway, I agreed to a price and began making plans for the future."

"Where will you go?"

"I have not decided, except I know I will leave Mexico. There is a change coming, and it will not be good for me or my family."

"In Arizona we hear talk of a revolution. Do you really think that there will be one?"

"I am sure of it. Don Porfirio's time in the sun has passed, though he refuses to admit it. My father's business did very well during his reign, but he can see the signs and he believes that when it does come, it will be violent and will go on for a long while. My family has survived for generations ... in fact, we prospered under many different leaders, but this time, the family is moving more of our investments out of Mexico. I have told my father that I want to be more involved in the family business, just as much as my brothers are, and he agrees that I should be. We have business interests in Europe and the United States, and my father and brothers want me to work in one of these places. I have been to France and Spain, and in my opinion, they are too much like Mexico in their views of women in business. I believe that I would have a slightly better chance in the States."

"Where in the States?" Owen felt his pulse quicken.

"We have interests in mining and ranching in New Mexico and California, and I would prefer to stay out west."

The richness and potential of her options were beyond Jones's comprehension. The little ranch he planned to buy was such a small thing that he was glad he had never mentioned it to her. He was excited by the possibility of her moving to the States, but at the same time, he felt something come between them. It was not so much a wall as a gap that grew wider the more he thought of it. But since he had first seen her, all reason and logic was being pushed out of him by his heart. He took his hat off and ran his finger around the inside of his hat band.

"I don't know what to think about you leaving Mexico, but I do know one thing for a fact. I would like to see you again." He looked at her and grinned, "and again."

She walked over to him and took his hat from his hands and looked directly into his eyes. What she saw convinced her beyond any doubt that she was right about him. She put her arms around his neck and kissed him full on the lips before hugging him and whispering in his ear, "You will see me again, Señor Jones. And again."

Jones arrived back at the colonel's hacienda at dusk and was met by Lieutenant Holguín, who informed the ranger that Sergeant Montaño and his group had located Mitchell's camp in the Sierras. The lieutenant also told him that they had received word that Mitchell and his gang had killed a village storekeeper and kidnapped his daughter.

"They found only one man there. He was very drunk but helpful in providing information on the gang and their activities. He named the gang members he knew and also verified your information about the incident with the women at the river. Miller and Bent are still with the gang. This man told Sergeant Montaño that Mitchell killed Mocho during an argument, and the two young ranch hands left the gang at the river. He also gave my men details about the murder of the storekeeper in the village and the kidnapping of his daughter. The sergeant and his men found her body in a canyon close to the camp. The man claims he had nothing to do with her or the women at the river."

"Does he know where Mitchell and his men are?" Jones asked.

"No. He said he woke up and they were gone but he is sure they are coming back. Sergeant Montaño agrees, so he and his men will fall back but keep an eye on the approaches to the camp."

Jones was quiet as he unsaddled his horse and carried the tack to the stable storeroom. "I'd give a month's pay to know what they are up to," he told the lieutenant.

"Yes, so would I, but whatever their plans, I believe they feel secure at their camp. It is remote, and the only people in that district live in a small village. The gang would never consider them a threat, and I am convinced that wherever they are or whatever their plans, they will return to the camp. From there, they could run north to the border or east to Chihuahua. I doubt they would go south to Yaqui country since there is nothing there for them."

"I hate the thought of waiting for them to do something," Jones said.

"I agree, as the does the captain, so it has been decided that I will take a *cordada* of *rurales* to the camp and wait for their return. The captain will remain here in command because the colonel is on his way to the capital. We have sent out notification to all points in the state to be alert for them. More than that we cannot do."

"When do we leave?" Jones asked.

"The men are preparing the equipment, supplies, and extra horses now." He instructed the stable groom to bring a fresh mount for Jones. "We will travel light and fast."

"And Ashley?" Jones asked.

"Juanito is with my men, helping with the preparations. I put him in charge of medical supplies." He smiled.

"Maybe this man the sergeant captured can give us more information about how many guns the gang has."

"I'm afraid that is impossible." The lieutenant shrugged his shoulders.

"Why?"

"Well, you see, he was shot while he was trying to escape."

"Ley fuga?" Jones asked.

"Yes. Ley fuga," Holguín said.

TWENTY-SIX

cLeod rode in the passenger car immediately behind the express car. According to railroad policy, the express car was placed behind the tender car so that it served as a barrier between the engine and the passenger cars. He sat with Mr. Church, the payroll manager, and his assistant, a man named Terwilliger. They occupied two rows of seats nearest the door leading to the express car. McLeod looked carefully at the other passengers in the car, trying to identify the members of Mitchell's gang. The car was about half full with a few businessmen, a large family, and, at the far end of the car, two roughly dressed men; one who was staring out the window and the other who was fast asleep. McLeod's imagination was very active since he had boarded the train in Hermosillo. He had never taken part in a robbery before and was frightened, but at the same time fascinated with the idea of how it would actually happen. Spence had not told him the whole plan, but that did not concern him because in all his dealings with Spence, the man had always told people just what they needed to know to carry out their part of the operation. McLeod was to sit with the mining company managers as he normally would and was to wait for

Mitchell and his men to make their move. They would treat him as just another company employee, and he was to do exactly as they told him. After it was over, he was to make his own way back to Hermosillo and then send word to Spence. Still, he could not help but wonder about how the gang would gain entrance to the express car. He knew the security men inside had strict orders not to open the doors except for the managers, who used a secret recognition signal.

McLeod's eyes continued to wander around the car. He noticed that one of the businessmen sat next to a very pretty young woman who looked directly at McLeod several times and smiled. McLeod would quickly look away when she did this, but when he casually looked back, she would still be looking at him. Is she in on it? he wondered. After a while, the movement of the train made him drowsy. He looked at the hard cases once again and saw that they were both asleep, so he leaned back against his seat and closed his eyes.

When they finally made their move, the gang did it quickly. McLeod opened his eyes to see four men with guns drawn. Two covered the passengers at the far end of the car, and the other two had their guns pointed at McLeod and the company managers. McLeod noticed that the two hard cases sat still with their hands raised along with the other passengers. The leader of the robbers, a dark and very stout man, not as tall as the others, knocked the manager's hat off his head and grabbed him by the hair. This must be Mitchell, thought McLeod.

"Let's go!" he demanded.

But Mr. Church, a stubborn man, resisted. "No! I won't!"

Mitchell nodded to his partner, an American. The American bandit pointed his pistol at Terwilliger and looked back at the leader.

"I said, let's go!" Mitchell pulled at Church's thinning hair.

"No! You can't ..."

Mitchell nodded once, and the American pulled the trigger of his revolver and blew Terwilliger's brains all over the seat and window. Church's eyes rolled back into his head as he fainted. Mitchell let go of his hair, and Church fell forward, wedging himself between the seat edge and the floor. Mitchell reached over the unconscious manager and grabbed McLeod by his jacket, pulling him over the seat into the aisle. The robber was powerfully built and lifted him like a small valise. Mitchell looked at McLeod with flat, cold eyes, and suddenly, the accountant was very afraid. The bandit pushed him to the door that led to the express car.

"There's a code!" McLeod shouted. He tried to turn his head and talk to Mitchell, but his neck was in the grip of a huge, powerful hand. "I don't know the code!" He was frantic.

He opened the door and stepped out onto the car's platform. Mitchell pushed him across onto the platform of the express car, and they were quickly joined by two more of the gang. These two crouched down out of sight in the area called the blind baggage, where they would be out of view of anyone in the express car. Still holding McLeod by the neck, Mitchell knocked on the heavy wooden door of the express car with the butt of his pistol.

"That you, Mr. Church?"

"It's McLeod!"

"What do you want? Where's Mr. Church?"

Mitchell let go of McLeod's neck. "How many inside?" He nodded toward the door.

"Three," McLeod answered.

"Tell them to open the peep hole!"

Before McLeod could respond, one of the guards slid a small wooden slat open and looked out at McLeod. He could not see the bandits but did see the look of terror on the accountant's face. "What the hell's going on, McLeod? Where's Mr. Church?"

"He's … they killed Terwilliger!" McLeod's voice was strained and high.

Mitchell pushed McLeod aside and looked into the peephole at the guard. "We'll start killing the others until you open up!'

The peephole slammed shut.

"Wait! They mean it!" McLeod shouted at the men in the express car.

Mitchell spoke to one of his men, who went back into the passenger car.

"Open the peephole and see for yourself!" Mitchell yelled.

Two of his men returned to the platform holding Terwilliger's body between them. They held him up so that what remained of his head was level with the peephole.

The guard slid the small slat open and looked into Terwilliger's dead face. "Sweet Jesus!" he yelled and slammed the peephole shut again.

Mitchell grabbed Terwilliger by the shirt front and tossed him off the platform. McLeod watched as the body hit the ground and then disappeared from sight as the train sped on. "All right, we're opening the door!" a voice yelled from inside the express car.

The heavy wooden door opened inward, and Mitchell, holding McLeod in front of him, entered first. The three guards stood with their hands in the air, and Mitchell called for the others to enter. They took the guard's weapons and led them back to the passenger car. Two more of the gang came into the express car and opened the front door. McLeod could see the tender car and, beyond that, the curved roof of the engine. The two men stepped out onto the platform and jumped up onto the tender. They drew their pistols and began making their way across the heaps of coal to the engine.

McLeod pointed out the cash boxes, and Mitchell's men immediately began smashing them open. There was a large safe in the car, but the men ignored this and concentrated on transferring the cash and coin from the strongboxes into canvas sacks they had brought with them. Another of the robbers who had gone to join the two on the tender returned and told Mitchell that the engine was in their control. Mitchell nodded and went over to the side door and slid it open. The cool air from the countryside flowed through the car, and McLeod realized that he was soaked with sweat as the breeze chilled him. He was impressed with the businesslike manner of the robbers as they went about transferring the money into the small canvas sacks that could be carried more easily on horses. Several of the robbers who had been in the passenger car returned with a large sack containing cash, jewelry, and guns that they had taken from the passengers. They began going through the loot and picked out the weapons. They put these in a separate bag.

Mitchell stepped out of the front of the car, crossed the platform, and climbed up onto the tender. He signaled to his men in the engine, and McLeod felt the train slow. In a short while, it came to a complete stop. Two of the men stepped down onto the rail bed and uncoupled the passenger cars and waved to Mitchell, who signaled to the engine. The train began to move again. The men laughed as they watched the rest of the cars fade in the distance. After fifteen or twenty minutes, the train slowed and once again came to a stop. McLeod heard some of the men laughing and shouting. He looked out the side door of the car and saw two men leading a string of saddled horses. The men immediately began taking the sacks from the express car to the horses. Two of outlaws marched the engineer and two of his assistants back to the express car. They tied their hands and feet with rope and stood them against the large safe and with a lariat rope lashed them securely to it. McLeod watched the robbers go about their business quietly and efficiently. In a very short time, the gang was mounted and ready to leave. The engineer looked at McLeod with wide, questioning eyes. McLeod turned and stepped down onto the rail bed. He did not want the train crew to hear any words spoken between him and Mitchell. He began walking over to Mitchell, who sat his horse out of sight of the car. McLeod was not sure what to say to the bandit chief. Everything had been worked out between Mitchell and Spence.

Mitchell sat and watched McLeod walk toward him and remembered the percentage of the loot that Spence insisted go to the little accountant. Mitchell thought it was far too much. He hated the fussy little man, but Spence had been firm in telling Mitchell that the man had played a large and important part in setting up the robbery. He watched the accountant's mincing steps as he approached the mounted group of men, and he could not bring himself to acknowledge that this creature was even a small part of his gang's activities.

McLeod sensed something in Mitchell's cold stare. He slowed and then stopped in his tracks when he saw Mitchell draw his pistol. He began backing up to the train and had taken three steps when Mitchell shot him in the stomach. McLeod doubled over but was amazed to find himself still standing. He turned and ran back toward the express car. He reached the open doorway and, with strength he did not know he possessed, he began to pull himself up into the car. He saw the wide, frightened eyes of the train crew. He hollered out to them.

"*Ayudame*!!" He felt lightheaded and began giggling as he realized the futility of asking for help from men who were bound to the three-quarter-ton safe. He was halfway into the car and still giggling when the second bullet hit him slightly off center in the upper back and tore through his heart.

Mitchell ejected the two spent casings and reloaded, and then he and the others turned their horses east and began their long ride back to the Sierras.

TWENTY-SEVEN

T he gang made good time after they crossed the rough ground and series of ravines that ran east of the rail line. They rode hard over a flat terrain and were halfway across the first low range of hills by late afternoon. Mitchell led them around several ranches in the adjoining valley, and they began their climb out of the lowlands into the mountains at dusk. He was satisfied that they had not been seen. He knew they left a wide and obvious trail but was not concerned. After they reached the main foothills of the Sierra, pursuit, if it came, would be slow and could easily be observed by the gang. Mitchell would rely on an old trick used by the Apaches and the Yaquis during their wars with the Mexican army.

The western slope of the Sierra in this region consisted of a series of long sloping ridges that ran like buttresses from the foothills up into the mountains. The pursued could either climb through the ravines, which were filled with scrub trees and undergrowth, or ride fully exposed on the bare ridges. They could not be seen in the ravines, but the climbing had to be done on foot and it was very slow going. Mitchell would ride the ridges like the Indians. By using the ridge crests, they could travel fast and any pursuers could be easily seen. The pursued could then set ambushes anywhere they chose. He knew that neither the army nor the *rurales* would follow him on the crests unless they had overwhelming numbers, and he was convinced they had not had time to gather such a force. The light of the moon in the cloudless sky gave him even more confidence, and he pushed hard for the foothills.

He was to meet Spence at the head of a ravine that opened onto a seasonal creek in the east of the valley. The ravine led to a path through a series of wooded hills to the base of the Sierras. He had given a considerable amount of thought to this meeting and had made up his mind to do what he had wanted to do for a long time. He would kill Spence, and he would do it quickly. He was not afraid of Spence, but he respected the man's ability to detect danger and his absolute ruthlessness in dealing with any and all threats. He had always hated the way Spence treated him, never as an equal but always as a peon who did his dirty work. He had been waiting for the right time and had decided that this was it. He didn't need Spence anymore and had considered how much more money he would have with both McLeod's and Spence's cuts.

The water ran shallow in the creek, not yet swollen with the winter runoff from the Sierras, and the stream rolled softly away from the hills, a shimmering blanket of ripples being pulled over its pebbled bottom. It made Mitchell sleepy, and he turned from it to look up the ravine and then up and down the banks that ran along the hills to his back. He sent men downstream to look for signs of Spence. The men rode several miles before turning back and reporting to their chief that they had found no signs. The moonlight on the creek and the breeze pushing through the scrub oak gave Mitchell a spooked feeling. It would be just like Spence to hide up there and wait for the right time to finish him off. The night breeze touched the back of his neck, and he gave the order to move out. He knew it would never be over with Spence until he killed him, but he could wait no longer. In his mind's eye, he could see the army moving quickly across the flatland west of this low range of hills, slowly but steadily following their tracks. He felt better as they rode into the ravine, but would not be confident until they reached the ridges of the Sierras. They had a long way to go.

In fact, there were no pursuers. Captain Amador had asked the army to scout north from Hermosillo to Magdalena, between the rail line and the Rio Sonora, looking for signs of the gang. He had told the army colonel that his *rurales* would move south on the east side of the river. He did not tell the cavalry officer about the bandit camp high in the Sierras, since the *rurales* could move more quickly and lightly in the mountains, and the captain's hard-riding veterans had the command and discipline it would require to lie in wait and carry out the ambush he had planned. He had sent a wire to the outpost at Nacozari, and they would dispatch a fast-riding courier to carry the news about the train robbery to Lieutenant Holguín. He smiled as he lit a small cigar. This would not change any of his plans for the ambush, he thought, but the news of the robbery and the killings would now allow Lieutenant Holguín and his men to finish it once and for all with this gang of murderers.

TWENTY-EIGHT

———◆———

The *cordada* of *rurales* led by Lieutenant Holguín pushed hard all night on their way to the gang's hideout. They made their rendezvous with Sergeant Montaño at a small village close to the Rio Bavispe just after dawn. The exhausted men unsaddled their mounts and led them to a small, shaded corral where they watered and fed them and gave them a quick rubdown. After a quick, cold meal, the men spread out their bedrolls and fell into a sound sleep.

The courier from Captain Amador was two hours behind them. He found Lieutenant Holguín, who was being briefed by Sergeant Montaño on his reconnaissance, and gave him the news of the train robbery.

"Now we know where they were." Holguín smiled. He then briefed his sergeant and the rangers on the contents of the message.

"How much time do we have before they return to their camp?" Jones asked.

"I would guess, if they rode hard, they will be at the hut by mid to late afternoon." The lieutenant looked at his sergeant.

"I agree. If we leave now, we can be there by noon or a little after," Sergeant Montaño said.

"All right, Sergeant. I hate to deprive the men of their beauty sleep, but we have no time to lose."

The sergeant grinned. "We will be ready to ride in ten minutes, *Teniente.*"

Lieutenant Holguín sent several fast-riding scouts ahead to the hut and instructed them to reconnoiter the area in case any of the gang arrived earlier than expected. He then led the rest of the troop out of the village and onto the trail, and they rode higher and deeper into the Sierras. Upon the return of one of the scouts, who confirmed that all was clear, the main body of *rurales* rode hard and arrived at the hut minutes before noon. Sergeant Montaño sent out a detail to cover all signs of the *cordada's* movement, even though they had approached from the direction opposite of where they expected the gang to arrive. The rest of the men gathered on a small hill overlooking the clearing in which the hut was located.

Lieutenant Holguín had the sergeant brief everyone on the results of his reconnaissance. The sergeant had drawn a diagram of the bandits' campsite on a large piece of paper; on another, he had sketched the surrounding area, marking all paths, ravines, and dry creek beds. All fields of fire were clearly marked. He then described the areas that offered cover and concealment for an ambush. Jones was impressed by Montaño's detailed answers for every one of the lieutenant's questions, and it was clear to him that they had carried out this exercise many times. There was a strong sense of confidence between them, but they were formal with each other, their questions and answers politely framed, as if they were trying hard not to cause offense in any way. Although Jones admired this polite approach and admitted that it was every bit as thorough as any briefing he had been party to, he had to fight the impulse to jump in and ask more direct and blunt questions. But he kept quiet, and he and Ashley absorbed the details of the briefing. As Lieutenant Holguín made the assignments, his sergeant carefully penciled them in on the map.

Jones and Ashley would be with the sergeant at the point nearest the hut, and the others would be positioned in a rough semicircle behind cover on the hill overlooking the hut.

The hut was built at the edge of a clearing in a small forest of pine and cedar. There was a ramshackle corral made of logs and rocks that sat opposite the hut, and a deep ravine twisted along the south side, gradually angling to the northeast about fifty yards behind the hut. From his position on the small, tree-covered hill directly across the clearing from the wooden building, Jones could see a large stand of trees and tangled undergrowth that ran from one side of the hut to the ravine. Sergeant Montaño told him there was no back door to the hut, but Jones calculated that if anyone managed to get to the trees, they had more than an even chance of escaping up the ravine. The ground on the far side of the ravine was open and bare of any trees or shrubs and ran on a good sixty yards to a tree line of scrub oak and pine. They were counting on the ravine itself to prevent any escape on horseback to the open ground on the other side, but if anyone made it into the ravine, they would not be stupid enough to run out of cover into an open field of fire.

Overall, Jones was satisfied with the plan to allow the gang into the clearing and then shut off any escape by covering the one path that entered the clearing, but he could not rid himself of the nagging thought of some of the outlaws making it to the woods between the hut and ravine. He swung the barrel of his rifle across the open field of fire from the front of the hut to the ravine. It would be a long run for someone under fire, but depending on the accuracy of that fire, it could be done. They could not put any of the men into the ravine because it was completely open to view from the approach up the trail. And to place anyone in the trees on the far side of the open ground would diminish the fire power needed from their ambush position. Not only that, they would be close to creating a cross-fire situation. So he accepted that the plan was as good as any under the circumstances. He called Ashley over, and they began to share out the .30 caliber ammunition for their Winchesters and then checked and double-checked their revolvers.

Jones continued to study the hut. He admired the solid log construction of the front and sides. The roof was in bad disrepair, and it looked like the hut had not been used in a long time. He remembered his plans for the building site on the small ranch east of Patagonia. The first time he had seen it, he had had a vision of building an adobe house with a flat roof. He would build it with the front facing south with a long covered porch at the entrance so he could sit there in the evening and watch the setting sun reflect off the Huachuca Mountains. It had taken root in his mind as much more of a real plan since he had talked to the banker, and as each week passed, he was more confident that he could do it. He had counted out how much he would need to invest in livestock and made a mental list of the material he would need to build the house, mend fences, and build corrals. He knew he had more than enough to make it happen. But a cloud floated over his thoughts when he thought about Catalina and his own plans. All of the other parts of his dream were achievable, but he just could not picture Catalina living on this small ranch in southern Arizona. He could not bring himself to even think about discussing it with her.

Jones thumbed the hammer of his revolver back to half cock and opened the cylinder gate. He moved the cylinder to expose the empty chamber on which the hammer had been resting and slid a fresh cartridge into the hole. Well, he thought, there is not a whole hell of a lot that can be accomplished by thinking and wishing. Besides, he had best keep his mind on the business at hand or he wouldn't be around to build any damn ranch house.

The sun was high above them, and they felt some of its warmth seep through the branches of the trees and soak through the clothing on their backs. After they had agreed that the gang would arrive by late afternoon, the lieutenant had sent scouts several miles down the trail. These scouts would relay word of the gang's approach back to the main body of men.

Sergeant Montaño had the bolt out of his Mauser and ran a rod very precisely down the barrel of the carbine. Jones admired the oiled wooden stock and the businesslike protrusion of the bolt. It was a fine rifle, and the Mexicans kept theirs clean and well oiled, but he did not know if it was the men's respect for the weapon or Montaño's constant inspection of their equipment that made them fastidious in their care for their rifles.

Sergeant Montaño nodded to Jones, and the two got up and walked out from behind their cover and down the rise to the clearing. Together, they tried to spot the hidden *rurales* from every angle of the clearing. They could see no reflections or shadows, nor could they hear any sounds, though they listened closely. The sun was beginning its arc to the west and would be close to the edge of the mountain horizon by mid to late afternoon, giving them the advantage of the sun at their backs. They climbed back to their hidden position, and then Montaño went to report to the lieutenant.

Jones lay prone and swung his rifle through his field of fire several times. When he was satisfied he had a clear, unobstructed view, he turned over and lay on his back. The mountain jays that had been disturbed when the troop of men had first arrived had settled down, and their chattering was back to normal. Their movements in the scrub cedar were abrupt flashes of bright blue as they darted about in their low-winged flight. Jones thought about the three killers he wanted: Mitchell, Bent, and Miller. He had made it clear to Ashley that these three were their top priority. They had discussed the arrest and transport of the three back to Arizona, but Jones knew they would fight, and he knew he would kill them. Maybe then, he thought, it would be over. After Sergeant Montaño returned, they went over the ambush plan one more time and reconsidered all the things that could go wrong. When Jones was satisfied that he had covered everything as best he could, he lay flat on his back and covered his face with his hat.

About three o'clock, word came from the scouts down the mountain that a gang of twelve men were on the trail heading for the hut. The lieutenant went to each position and checked on his men. His plan was to allow the gang to enter the clearing, dismount, and unsaddle their mounts. His men were to wait until the horses were corralled and the gang had begun to relax, and he would then call on the bandits to surrender. If there were any moves on the part of the gang to resist, if any of them even reached for a weapon, his men were to open fire.

The clearing was a mix of bright sunlight and long, dark shadows, and Jones knew that when the sun, which was at his back, went behind the mountain peaks, it would get dark quickly. He was studying the strip of sunlight that lit up the door of the hut when the sounds of men riding up the trail reached him. As the first group of men rode into the clearing, he searched for Bent and Miller among them. He did not spot them, and then he smiled as he remembered Mitchell's cunning. He was letting his men lead on the narrow mountain trails where a trap could easily be set. All it would take would be a lack of discipline or one anxious shooter, and Mitchell would be off back down the trail, but the *rurales* were a hard, disciplined crew, and the only sounds in the clearing were the calls of the mountain jays in the trees.

As all of the gang came into view, Jones counted twelve men and noted that his three were the last to enter the clearing. He knew that the trail would be closed by the detail of *rurales* assigned that task; anyone who attempted to escape back down the trail would be cut to pieces. He watched the men dismount. They were quiet and didn't engage in the usual banter of men returning to camp after a long ride. They were exhausted, and they moved slowly as they unsaddled their mounts and led them over to the makeshift corral. Several men lay down in the pine needles under the trees at the edge of the clearing. Mitchell and the two Americans carried canvas sacks and saddlebags into the hut.

"*Atención!*" Lieutenant Holguín's deep voice shattered the stillness in the clearing. "We are *rurales*, and you are all under arrest! Put down your guns and raise your hands!"

Jones held the front sight of his Winchester on the sunlit square of the hut's door. In his peripheral vision, he saw several of the bandits move quickly toward the tree line. He heard the loud reports of the *rurales'* Mausers, and now there was no doubt and there were no options for the gang. The outlaws who were not cut down in the first round of fire took cover and began returning fire. Jones heard the rounds snap above his head and smack into the trees. The bandits were firing blindly in the general direction of the *rurales'* positions. Their shots were going high, but if they were worth their salt, that would soon change. Three of the outlaws ran across the front of the hut and through his sights, but he held his fire because they were not who he wanted. They were running for the ravine. Jones was still focused on the door of the hut, but out of the corner of his eye, he saw Sergeant Montaño move out from behind his cover and slide down the hill to the clearing. Jones lost sight of Montaño behind several large pine trees but heard the sergeant's Mauser and saw one of the men fall. The other two men ran on toward the ravine, firing blindly back in the direction of the sergeant. Ashley had moved over to Jones's right and down the rise behind the trees to cover the sergeant. Jones heard him yell, "Montaño is down!"

"Wait!" Jones yelled back and immediately rolled over and got to his feet. He moved quickly down the hill and joined Ashley, who had taken up a covering position behind a tree. Sergeant Montaño lay face down about twenty-five feet beyond the trees in the clearing. Dust spurted up around him as the bandits tried their best to put more lead into him. Jones laid his Winchester next to Ashley.

"When you see me break cover, keep their heads down." He spoke calmly to Ashley.

Ashley pulled Jones's rifle closer to him and nodded. Jones slid a little further down the hill behind the trees and reached a spot about ten yards from the fallen sergeant. He could see the sergeant breathing and saw a dark stain on the back of his jacket. Montaño's Mauser was in the dirt two or three feet in front of him, but he held his revolver in his right hand. Jones stood up straight behind the tree. He drew his revolver and turned his face up the hill.

"OK, J.T.!" he yelled. He heard Ashley's Winchester open a steady rhythm, and he ran out from behind the tree to Montaño. He heard rounds snap past his head and saw dirt and rocks kick up around him. He returned fire with his Colt as he ran into the clearing. He reached Montaño, grabbing him by the collar of his short jacket and dragging him back to the trees, aiming his Colt at the outlaws. Jones felt Montaño's weight ease a bit and saw that the sergeant was pushing with his legs against the ground. The sergeant raised his revolver and began firing at the outlaws. With Jones's load lightened, they moved more quickly. Jones turned to look back at the trees when he felt a sharp blow to his right leg just before he fell flat on his back. He and the sergeant both lay there for a moment, stunned, and they saw one of the men who had been shooting at them rise up and aim his carbine at them. Jones heard the sharp crack of a Winchester behind him and to his left and saw the outlaw drop his carbine and fall backwards.

"Let's go, sergeant!" Jones grabbed Montaño, and they both began scrambling backwards like two crabs locked together.

They reached the trees, and Montaño crawled around behind a large cedar and propped himself up. Jones lay on his stomach behind a large rock and looked across the clearing. He saw an outlaw jump up and begin running toward the ravine. Again, Jones heard Ashley's Winchester and saw the outlaw drop in his tracks. He rolled over and ran his hand down his leg, checking for damage. His leg was numb, but everything felt fine until his hand reached his boot top. He felt the wetness and knew that he had been hit but could not tell how badly. He crawled over to Montaño, who was now unconscious, and saw Ashley scrambling down the hill carrying two Winchesters. Ashley handed Jones his rifle and turned to the sergeant. He pulled the sergeant's jacket and shirt down and examined the wound.

"There's an exit wound and no real serious bleeding." He turned to Jones. "Let's have a look at your leg."

Jones lay on his stomach and covered the clearing with his rifle while Ashley cut at the cuff of his trousers with a knife. There was no pain, but he could feel Ashley picking around the back of his lower leg.

"Whatever it was went clear through," Ashley said. He wrapped a large bandage tightly around Jones's leg and then lay prone next to Jones. They looked across the clearing to the hut and saw smoke starting to pour from the holes in the dilapidated roof. All shooting had stopped. Jones and Ashley looked at each other, wondering what was happening. They heard the slide of loose rock as someone came sliding down the hill behind them.

It was Lieutenant Holguín and several of his men.

Ashley briefed them on Montaño's wound as one of the men opened a medical kit and began pulling out clean dressings. Ashley helped the man clean the wound, and they applied the dressings and rigged a sling for the sergeant's arm. Jones was concentrating on the hut and saw the door flung suddenly open. Three men rushed out, firing their pistols and running for the trees in the direction opposite of the ravine. The *rurales* opened fire, and at the same time, three more men burst out of the hut and ran for the undergrowth and the ravine. These three did not waste time firing at the *rurales* and were soon out of sight in the undergrowth. Jones saw that it was Mitchell and the two Americans. He immediately got up and began running across the clearing in a straight line for the ravine. He felt his heart pumping, and the numbness in his leg was replaced by a pain that became more intense as he ran. He focused on the three men and climbed down over the rocks to the floor of the ravine, trying to estimate the point at which the men would break out of the brush. He quickly made his way over the rocks and small boulders in their direction. He gritted his teeth against the pain in his leg and moved toward a low wall of boulders that spilled across the bottom of the ravine. He made his way around the boulders on the side away from the hut and stopped to adjust his eyes to the shadowed light of the undergrowth where he reckoned the men would make their break. He felt a hard blow and a sharp sting on his cheek below his left eye, then he heard the report of a revolver down the ravine. He ducked behind the boulder wall and felt his cheek. No bullet, he thought, rock chips. He counted to three and then pushed himself up and away from the boulder on his left. He saw three men running away from him up the ravine. He brought his rifle to his shoulder and drew a bead on the man at the tail end and squeezed the trigger. The man fell forward on his face, his arms spread out as if he were trying to fly. Jones levered another round into the chamber of the Winchester.

That's one, he thought and began moving up the ravine. As he approached the fallen outlaw, he heard the man groan. The outlaw's right hand still gripped his revolver. Jones drew his Colt and thumbed back the hammer. He slowed as he passed to the right of the outlaw, aimed his Colt at the man's head, and put a bullet in his brain.

Jones moved quickly up the narrowing canyon. He had to keep moving. If he stopped, he knew that his leg would stiffen up on him. His cheek began to swell, and his left eye was beginning to close from the bottom up. He heard Ashley and the lieutenant calling him from behind. They were close, judging from the strength of their voices. As the ravine narrowed, there were fewer boulders, and the going was easier. He could hear the two bandits scrambling through the loose rock ahead of him, and as he came to a turn, he saw only one man who stood, a grin on his face, as he pointed his pistol at Jones. Jones ducked behind a rock as the outlaw fired. He heard the scrambling of feet slipping on loose rock, but when he looked again, the outlaw was gone.

Jones holstered his Colt and moved to his right and began to climb the wall of the ravine, trying to get up on the clear ground so he could get a better view up the ravine. As he reached the top, he grabbed at the edge with his right hand and pulled himself up and over, his rifle in his left hand. He swung over the edge of the ravine and at the same time felt like someone had hit his left hand with a crowbar. The Winchester swung back and hit him on the forehead. His vision blurred, and as he reached for his holster, he saw Mitchell up on the rocky clear ground, about halfway to the stand of scrub oak and pine trees. Mitchell was aiming his rifle at Jones. Jones grabbed his Colt, but the ring and little fingers of his right hand had clasped themselves firmly to his palm. He fumbled at the grip of the Colt with his other two fingers and his thumb. He ducked back down over the edge of the ravine just as Mitchell fired. Rocks and dirt flew over his head, and he rolled to his right, pulling on the contracted fingers with his left hand. He kept rolling and finally got a firm grip on the revolver. He pushed himself up over the edge and saw Mitchell running for the trees. He cocked the Colt, holding it with both hands, held low, and squeezed the trigger. He saw Mitchell go down. He re-cocked the pistol and fired again. Mitchell was down, but he was crawling to the trees.

Blood ran freely down Jones's forehead and into his eyes, and he heard Ashley and Holguín on his right and thought he saw some figures dressed in white led by a bearded old man come out of the trees near where Mitchell lay. He wiped at the blood with his left hand and looked again. They were still there, and now they were dragging Mitchell away from the clearing into the brush. Jones cocked the Colt and raised it to eye level.

"No! Jones! No!" the lieutenant yelled.

"Hold your fire, Owen!" Now it was Ashley giving him orders, he thought.

"What the hell?" he yelled at them.

The men in white were dragging Mitchell into the trees just as Holguín and Ashley reached him.

"It's OK, Owen. Sit down now. Take it easy now." Ashley's voice was soothing and helped make the red mist fade from Jones's mind.

"Who were they?" Jones asked as he sat down. His leg was on fire, and he was getting dizzy and thought he would be sick.

"They are old friends," the lieutenant said.

"Oh! All right, then!" Jones heard his voice from far away. I can't see, he thought, and now I'm losing my hearing. He thought about the ghost-like figures in white coming out of the woods and wondered about death. Ashley was speaking to him, but his voice was distant, fuzzy-like. Jones closed his eyes, but he saw bright flashes. It's all pretty damn strange, he thought. And just before he lost consciousness, he heard, very distinctly, loud, sobbing screams coming from the trees. The screams echoed sharply across the broken rocks on the clear ground above the ravine.

TWENTY-NINE

⸻◆⸻

D r. Lovato studied the papers in his hand, and in a professional, almost cold manner, began to describe the extent
of his patient's injuries. Jones, who had resigned himself
to the doctor's strict orders for a week's bed rest, listened
with all the stoicism he could muster.

"The leg is healing nicely. You were very fortunate that the bullet went through cleanly without hitting bone or major blood
vessels. I cleaned out a small amount of clothing debris, and you
suffered no infection in this wound. The face became infected
from slivers of rock, but we removed them all, and that is also
coming along nicely. You will, of course, have a scar since I could
not close the wound while it was infected. I closed the wound on
your forehead with twelve sutures and will remove them next
week. The worst of your problems is that your brain was concussed when your rifle struck you." The doctor paused and gave
Jones a tight smile. "It would have been much worse if the bullet
hit you instead of your rifle. So my only real concern is with the
head. You cannot travel for a while, and as I told you earlier, I
insist on bed rest for another week. Any questions?"

"What's wrong with my hand, Doc?" Jones held up his right hand. "My fingers want to close in on my palm. Damn near cost me back there in the Sierras. I couldn't grip my Colt."

The doctor took Jones's hand and worked the ring and little fingers and felt a knot under their base in the palm. "How long has it been like this?"

"Couple of years. Mostly just cramps. But it's been getting worse lately."

"It is called Dupuytren's Contracture, and without boring you with the details, I can tell you that it won't get any better, only worse. Eventually, the fingers will lock against the palm. There is a surgical procedure, but I would not recommend it. I will make you a splint that you can wear at night or whenever it is that you have no need of your firearm." The doctor continued to probe the skin of Jones's hand. He rubbed firmly against the knuckles of the right hand, straightening the fingers and then raising the hand to his ear, listening carefully as he manipulated the joints. He then grabbed the left hand and repeated this procedure. He put the hand down and gently felt the old scar tissue at Jones's brows and corners of his eyes.

"Mr. Jones? Did you practice the art of pugilism in the past?"

"Yes, I was a prize fighter when I was young."

Dr. Lovato shook his head. "I can tell you this, Mr. Jones. Rheumatism will eventually set in on both hands, and when that happens, the contracture will be the least of your worries. Also, there is no way of measuring any previous damage to the brain as a result of blows you may have received during your boxing career. So, if you sustain any additional blows to the head during your current career, well, let's just say your career could very well be drastically cut short."

Jones was quiet. He could not think of anything to say. "If I go to the trouble of making you a splint, will you wear it?" The doctor looked down at Jones from the high horse only a doctor can ride.

"Will it help?" Jones's head ached.

"It will help postpone the permanent closing of the fingers, yes."

"Then I'll do it."

"Anything else?" Dr. Lovato pulled out his watch.

"No. It's just that the thought of being cooped up sticks in my craw."

"Mr. Jones! You are fortunate to be alive, and if you do not do as I advise, you will court the possibility of serious brain damage. So if I were you, I would weigh the consequences very thoroughly."

"I didn't mean to seem ungrateful, Doc. I appreciate all you've done, and I will follow your advice to the letter." Jones held out his right hand, and the doctor shook it. "By the way, how is Sergeant Montaño?"

"He is doing fine, and I expect a full recovery." Dr. Lovato put his watch away. "Mr. Jones, you may not find your stay in our hospital as onerous as you might imagine." The doctor grinned mysteriously at Jones before leaving the room.

Jones gently touched his cheek and felt the large swelling. He moved his hand to his forehead and felt the stiff ends of the stitches over a good-sized knot. He looked around the room for a mirror but could not find one. He sighed and lay back on his pillow, trying to remember details of the action at the hut in the Sierras.

There was a gentle knock on the door, and before he could respond, it opened slowly. Catalina entered, holding a tray of food. He felt his heart jump as she came over and set the tray on a stand next to his bed. She reached out and grabbed his hand. Jones felt her warmth and realized what the doctor had meant about his stay.

"I could not stay down south when I heard you were here. I hope you don't mind, but I had to come. I am staying with Fermin, that is, Dr. Lovato, and his family. They are old friends and, oh, Owen! I was so afraid when I heard you were hurt." She spoke in a rush, trying to get all the words out.

He grabbed her hands with both of his. "You are beautiful!" he said. "And I'm glad you're here. I've thought about you every day since I last saw you."

She kissed him softly and regained her composure. "I could not bear the thought of losing you before I even got to know you. After you rode back to the colonel's that day, I thought of all the things I wanted to say to you."

Jones felt better. His headache was gone. "Careful, you'll give me a swelled head!"

She giggled and touched his face. "I'm afraid it's too late for that."

He groaned. "I must look like hell. I looked for a mirror but couldn't find one."

"No need for a mirror. And I don't care how you look. I am just glad you are here."

He watched her as she prepared the food on the tray and thought about the time they would spend together, and he had to agree with Dr. Lovato that he was indeed a very fortunate man.

The next evening, Colonel Kosterlitsky, Captain Amador, Lieutenant Holguín, Sergeant Montaño, and Ashley visited him. Ashley pushed Sergeant Montaño in a wheelchair. The colonel carried a gift-wrapped box and stood at the foot of the bed as the others gathered around.

The colonel spoke in his clipped military manner. "It is my honor to bring you the compliments of President Díaz and his best wishes for a speedy recovery." He stopped and looked at the others, and his voice softened. "And I speak for myself and all of my men when I thank you for your valiant behavior during the fight with the gang of bandidos in the Sierras. As a small token of our gratitude and esteem, we wish to present you with this gift."

He handed the box to Lieutenant Holguín, who pulled his knife out of its scabbard and handed it and the box to Jones. The ranger cut through the satin ribbon, carefully unwrapped the expensive-looking paper, and opened the box. He pulled out the most beautiful hand-tooled set of boots he had ever seen. He held them up and admired the seal of the Republic of Mexico stamped into the boot tops. The colonel came around the bed and shook Jones's hand.

"I have been in contact with Captain Wheeler, and I told him I could not send you home until you regain your strength and are as healthy as you were when you came to Mexico. *Salud,* amigo!"

The others each came over and shook Jones's hand and wished him well. He promised Sergeant Montaño he would stop by and visit him soon, and after some joking back and forth, they all left except Ashley. Jones handed him the boots, and Ashley put them on the floor next to the nightstand.

"Fine boots. I suppose you'll want to put them on as soon as possible." Ashley looked admiringly at the boots.

"Yep. But the doc says I got to stay here another week."

"He's right, Owen. A concussed brain is very serious, and it's just pure luck that your hand wasn't blown off. Mitchell's round hit your Winchester just above the trigger. It's completely ruined."

"I'm a little fuzzy about what happened back there, J.T. I remember some men dragging Mitchell to cover and hearing you tell me to hold my fire, but I can't quite put it all together."

"You did see men drag Mitchell off. They were men from the village. You remember? The village where they killed the storekeeper and kidnapped and killed his daughter? Well, they were dragging him off, all right, but they weren't taking him to cover. That's why we told you not to shoot. I saw his body later. The villagers got their revenge."

"You're sure it was Mitchell?"

"Very sure. Pete was right about the skin between his toes."

"And Zeke Bent?" Jones asked.

"Don't know." Ashley shook his head. "We tracked him back up the ravine and out onto some flats but lost the trail in the rocks farther up the mountain. Lieutenant Holguín is sure that he won't last long up there. It's already started to snow up higher, and there's nothing but Indians and mountain lions living up there. He's without a mount a long way from the border. I'd have to agree with Holguín about his chances."

"And what about the others?" Owen asked.

"All the others are dead. Miller was in the ravine where you dropped him, and we found two more in the hut. I'm not sure if they were wounded earlier, because they were pretty well destroyed by the fire. It looks like they started the fire as a diversion to draw attention away from them running out into the open. One thing is sure, the hut burned to the ground, and except for a few hundred in coins, everything else burned up. There were some paper bills left in the hut but we can't make out whether they forgot them or were left there for someone else to pick up on their way out. Several of them that were half burnt blew out of the hut and we found then in the clearing. Zeke Bent may have gotten away with some of the loot, because we didn't find any on Mitchell or Miller. And except for you and the sergeant, none of the *rurales* were even scratched." Jones was quiet, trying to recall the action and its aftermath, but except for some vague memories of being loaded into a wagon and riding in a train, he could not remember much.

"I do remember you giving me laudanum but can't recall much else."

"I loaded you and the sergeant up with the stuff. We knew it would be a rough trip down." Ashley picked up the boots again. Jones recognized the nervousness. "That brings me around to what I wanted to talk to you about."

"Something important, J.T.?"

"Well, yes. At least for me it is. I've decided to leave the Rangers and return to California to finish medical school." He looked at Jones, searching for his approval.

"And the girl?" Jones asked.

"We've been in touch. I realized that I really love her, and I asked her to marry me. I mean … it won't happen until after I get my degree."

"I'm happy for you, J.T. Happy and proud. You've been a good partner and a damn fine ranger. No doubt in my mind you'll be a damn fine doctor, too!"

"I'm glad you approve, Owen, because I gave it a lot of thought. I've killed three men in the last few months, and I know I was carrying out my duties, but, well, I just don't like killing, and I don't think I can do it again."

"You made a good choice, J.T. Pretty near any broken-down old cowhand can be a lawman, but it takes a special man to be a sawbones."

"Well, I don't know about that, but I've got a special favor to ask of you."

Jones raised his eyebrows and looked at the younger man.

"I haven't known you for very long, but we have been in situations that can never be matched. I mean nobody I know can even imagine it, and I could never begin to try to explain it to them. Anyway, I want to ask you to stand up for me at the wedding."

"You mean be your best man?"

"Yes."

"Why, J.T., I'd be proud to do it!"

"Thanks, Owen. I couldn't imagine asking anyone else." Ashley started to share more of his plans, but he could see the fatigue in the older ranger's face. "Well, you get some rest now. I'll stop by to see you tomorrow before I catch my train."

"Goodnight, J.T. See you tomorrow." Jones lay back on his pillows and was asleep before Ashley quietly closed the door.

Several evenings later, a priest came to visit Jones. "Hello, Padre, what can I do for you?"

"I heard there was a North American Catholic in our hospital, and I had to come see if it was true since most of you I have met were Protestant." The priest smiled. He was a small man, with a clean-shaven, pleasant face.

"Actually, I'm a Catholic by accident and I haven't been to Mass in years."

"I am sorry to hear that." The priest took on a scolding air. "What do you mean by accident?"

"I was raised by Jesuits in a foundling home, so I had no choice."

"The Jesuits! Well, they have been known to make life tedious, but I am a Franciscan, and we are a bit more forgiving. Is there anything I can do for you?"

"Thanks, Padre, but no. Dr. Lovato is taking good care of me, and I'm getting three squares a day. Nothing to complain about. Anyway, I'll be leaving soon."

"Three squares?"

"Meals, Padre."

"Oh, I see. Actually, I was thinking more of your spiritual needs."

"Like confession?"

"Well, yes, and …"

"No thanks, Padre. I know full well that I am not without sin, and I've sure broken my share of the commandments, but that's between me and God, and I decided long ago that I don't need a middleman. No offense."

"No offense taken." The priest studied Jones for a moment, the pleasantness returning to his face. "I was told you were very formidable, and I must agree; however, I don't need your permission to bless you or pray for you, so I will do both." He made the sign of the cross and turned to go. "Goodbye, my son. *Vaya con Dios!*"

"Thanks, Padre." Jones watched the priest leave and sighed. He turned to the window and was thinking about the priest's visit when Catalina knocked at the door and came into the room. Jones looked at her with a quizzical frown on his face.

"Did you send the priest?"

"Yes. I hope you are not upset."

"No, I guess I'm not, but it was a waste of his time."

"Actually, he enjoyed meeting a Catholic from the States, even if you are not a practicing Catholic." She came over and sat in the chair next to the bed and held his hand. "Fermin says you can get out of bed and start walking a little this evening."

"Good! I was going to get up and hobble around anyway."

She picked up the boots and looked at them admiringly. "Owen, I don't mean to pry, but you have never talked about your family. Are they still alive? Were you named after your father? What is your mother like? Is—"

"Whoa! Slow down, woman," he laughed. "I'm not trying to hide anything. It's just that, well, the family part of my life was long ago and such a small part that I don't ever think of it much. Now, what do you want to know?"

"What I just said, your name and the rest."

"All right, here it is. I was named after my uncle, my father's brother. My father's name was Patrick."

"Was?"

"Both he and my uncle were killed at Sharpsburg, where they were serving under General Hays. I was two years old. My mother's name was Angeline. The family had a small plantation north of Baton Rouge, but after Vicksburg was taken, the place fell apart and my mother took me to New Orleans, where we moved in with some relatives. I guess that didn't work out, because she took me to a foundling home and went off and killed herself. I learned all this from one of the Jesuit brothers in the home. So that's pretty much the family story."

"And you were raised in the home?"

"Yep. Not much else to say. I left the home when I was four-teen and earned a living working on the docks and fighting in bare-knuckle bouts on Sundays. Saved some money, got a ride on a steamer to Galveston, and here I am thirty-odd years later."

"Owen, the first day I met you, I asked how you dealt with the uncertainty. I know I promised not to ask again, but I must know what you think of these things."

"I have thought about the question, Catalina, and all I can tell you is there has never been any uncertainty. In fact, I think of it as pure and clear certainty."

"How?"

"It's not complicated. They break the law. I hunt them down. If they choose to fight, then there's a good chance I will kill them. Or they will kill me. Either way, it does not change the fact that I am in the right and they are in the wrong. That's the certainty of it all."

"They almost killed you this time! And just the thought of it makes me sad to think of what a waste it would be. Your life for theirs. It does not seem fair."

Jones was quiet. He did not know how to respond. He never thought of it in terms of fairness. Hell, life wasn't fair, and this was his life. He could not imagine any other life except for ranching. He had always tried to balance the rights and wrongs, but he knew better than to expect things to end up being fair.

"You like this life, then?" Her voice was soft.

"Yes, I do."

She had held his hand all the while she was talking, and when he was finished, she leaned over and kissed him. She then got up and walked over to the window. "Are you strong enough to walk?" she asked, her back to him.

"Yep. I'm feeling much stronger today."

"Good, wait one moment." She held up her hand.

The brightness of the room was fading with the evening light, and the hills behind the town were barely visible. Catalina walked over to the door. Owen heard the click of the lock, and then she came over and stood at the side of the bed. Her eyes locked on his, and very calmly and slowly, she took off her clothes and climbed into bed with him.

Jones hobbled around the hospital for a week, wearing Dr. Lovato's splint on his hand. He visited Sergeant Montaño every day, and the two lawmen developed a close friendship that would forever be cemented in the episode at the mountain hut. On the first visit, Jones had offered to push Montaño in his wheelchair, but the sergeant had stood up from his bed and weakly pushed the wheelchair into the corner of the room.

"No, they will not get me in that thing again!"

So once a day, they walked out to the central veranda, where they would sit and enjoy the late-autumn sun and swap stories that would never be shared with anyone who did not wear a badge.

On Jones's last night at the hospital, Catalina brought a tray with a special meal and a bottle of wine.

"The wine is from Fermin's own wine cellar," she said. "He is satisfied that the risk of infection is over and you are free to go at any time."

The food was excellent, as all the meals had been since Catalina had arrived. Jones was becoming accustomed to fine meals, and before long, he thought he might just become fat and happy. He did not know whether it was the wine or just the pleasure of her company, but he began to tell her about his plans for his small ranch just outside of Patagonia. He described the quality of the acreage and the grasses and the building site and his plans for the ranch house and how he planned to make use of the stream.

"It would be a pleasure to see this place. Will you take me there?" she asked.

"Yes, of course. It's a ways out and we'll have to camp out two or three nights. Would you mind?"

"I look forward to it. I was going to tell you earlier, but I will be in Phoenix in late January or early February. Will you meet me then?"

They made arrangements to contact each other and meet in Phoenix. It was not like Jones to plan that far ahead, but there was a growing possibility of a different future for him, and he felt an equal amount of apprehension and excitement as they made plans for the new year.

In the early dawn as she was dressing, Catalina looked down at the sleeping ranger, and she fought the urge to wake him. His face looked broken and scarred in the stark moonlight, and she remembered how shocked she had been when she had first seen him here in this room. His face had been red and so swollen that she had had trouble maintaining her composure until she had seen his eyes. They had been so full of the joy of seeing her that she had fallen in love all over again. He was not like the others in her world. He was not a polished gentleman, but he was gentle in other ways. He came from a world so different from hers, rough and hard, but perhaps that was the source of his honesty. She took delight in the simple joy and happiness that was so plain on his face when he talked of certain things. Like his dreams for the ranch and of Ashley asking him to be his best man. She thought that a man like this should have had children, lots of children, and had briefly imagined being married to him and bearing more children. But she quickly dismissed the idea as she faced the reality of their lives. She had grown accustomed to her independence since the death of Ernesto, and as time went by, she found herself jealously guarding the freedom to make choices for herself and Maria Cristina. She had never in her life let anyone dictate terms to her, but during the past year, she had become even more stubborn and could not imagine allowing another man into her world. She was forced to admit that she was confused because she so greatly cherished her time with Owen and the way he made her feel.

She liked the way he held her after they made love, as if he were trying to hold on to the bond of their passion for more than just the moment. It was as if their lovemaking was not enough, and she held him, not wanting him to let her go. She knew that he would be gone from her life in an instant if she tried to direct or influence him, but in an odd way, this was the basis of her hope because she was certain that he realized the same about her. She would pray that they would see each other again, for she was weary of the sadness that was expected of her as a widow and wanted more of the love she felt when they were together. She looked down at him once again and went over to the nightstand and wrote quickly on a note pad: "See you in Phoenix!" before quietly walking to the door. She knew she had to leave for the ranch before he woke. She needed to put distance between them, for she feared she would weaken and cling to him, and she knew that neither of them wanted that.

Early the next morning, Jones was packing his grip when Sergeant Montaño came into his room, carrying a rifle.

"Juanito asked me to give this to you before you left." He handed it to Jones.

It was a brand-new Winchester '95. Jones stood, staring at it.

"He said to tell you that it was to replace the one you lost in the Sierras." The sergeant laughed. "And this is from me." He handed Jones a fresh box of .30-.40 ammunition for the rifle.

Jones felt a lump in his throat and found he could do nothing but shake his head. He turned and fussed with his grip until he felt he could speak.

"Thank you, compadre. It means a lot to me."

Jones grabbed his grip and, carrying his new rifle, he walked with Montaño to the central veranda, where they said goodbye. Jones walked slowly over to Dr. Lovato's office and thanked him for everything. The doctor checked Jones's healing wounds one more time, wished him the best of luck, and called for the hospital buggy to take Jones to the train station. Jones sat back in the carriage as they drove slowly down the main streets of Cananea to the depot. It was a beautiful day with just a touch of winter chill finding its way down from the Sierras.

THIRTY

---◆---

The chief auditor was not well. He hated being here in Mexico and considered his accommodations at the Cananea mine site to be uncivilized. His bowels cramped, and he had not had solid food for several days. He had been living on clear broth and blue pills that were supposed to stop the cramping. In fact, they gave him very little relief, but his spirits had been lifted by a telegram he had received from the company president.

Shortly after the chief auditor had begun his examination of the company books, it had become apparent that McLeod had been billing the company through a series of nonexistent companies. Although the fictitious contractors and companies had been cleverly concealed, the chief auditor's thorough examination had revealed the scheme in its entirety. He had looked forward to questioning McLeod, only to learn that the little thief had been killed by a gang of train robbers while he was returning to the mine with the company payroll.

At first, the chief auditor had felt cheated and was very disappointed, but then in a moment of inspiration, a wonderful opportunity emerged from the misfortune of death and the stolen payroll. He had wired his idea, carefully worded, to the president and had received his answer that very morning. The telegram was brief and to the point:

Agree with your plan—Your figures too low—Add more to include Colorado—Work on more figures on return trip—Will finalize details here—Return immediately—Stop

The fact that he would finally be leaving this miserable place and returning to civilization eased some of the strain on the chief auditor's bowels, and he made arrangements to leave on the next train. He envisioned a good bonus for his work in uncovering the fraud that would be known only to the president and himself, but his real value in this matter was his plan to blend the losses of the Colorado operation into an inflated figure of the lost but insured payroll. The amount of the loss would, as usual, be negotiated with the underwriter, but he was certain that his contacts in the insurance company would settle on a figure that would be very favorable to him.

The chief auditor's spirits lifted, and the cramping in his gut subsided as he packed his bags and called for an assistant to take him to the train station. He imagined himself arriving in New York something of a conquering hero and allowed himself the thought of fine meal laid out at the Waldorf. He immediately regretted this when his bowels cramped in rejection of even the thought of solid food.

———

Eugenia del Castillo brought a bottle of champagne and waited impatiently in Spence's suite of rooms. She had opened the champagne and drunk several glasses while waiting. He was one of the most interesting and challenging lovers she had known, but she was growing tired of their relationship. She planned to make this her last meeting with him and then would simply, as she had with past lovers, cease to acknowledge him in the future.

Her fingers touched the front of her throat, and she frowned at the absence of her pearl necklace. In spite of a thorough and frantic search of her suite, she could not find it, even though she remembered wearing it when she had returned to her rooms. She carried her glass of champagne as she wandered around Spence's suite. In the bedroom, she saw his traveling alarm clock on the nightstand and noted that there were several suits hanging in the armoire. She went back into the sitting room and flounced down on the sofa. Where the hell was he? She was not accustomed to being kept waiting and had made up her mind to leave if he had not arrived by the time she finished one more glass of champagne.

Jones was assigned to light duty, and all of December and the first two weeks of January were spent helping with administrative duties at Ranger headquarters while his wounds healed. The holidays came and went without incident, and in the second week of the new year, Jones paid a visit to Dr. Howard J. Biesecker. The doctor had his offices and surgery in the front of an old wood-frame house on South Gieseler Avenue. Jones still walked with a slight limp and used the railing alongside the steps to help himself up onto the porch. The doctor himself let Jones in when he knocked at the door. There were no patients, and the doctor did not have a staff to assist him. Jones introduced himself, and the doctor showed him into the office while studying the healing wounds on Jones's face.

"What can I do for you, Ranger?"

"I have some questions for you about an investigation I'm conducting. I realize some of the questions may be covered by the rules of doctor-patient relationship, but you may be able to clear up some things for me."

"Glad to do what I can, but from the looks of you, I thought you may have required my professional attention. May I ask what happened to you?"

Jones explained how he had received the wounds and then provided the details of his investigation and the discovery and examination of the remains of the MacDuff women. The doctor asked questions about the manner of the women's deaths and the condition of their remains. Jones handed him Dr. Lovato's report and studied him closely as he read it and then reread it.

"A very thorough and professional examination, but what is it you want of me?" The doctor leaned back in his chair.

"Before I talk to Mr. MacDuff, I wanted to ask you, since you attended the family, what you could tell me about the young girl's broken bones and what you might know about any ill treatment of her."

Dr. Biesecker sighed and picked up his pipe from an ashtray on his desk. "Yes, I attended the girl's injuries." The doctor rubbed his eyes. "Have you seen MacDuff lately?"

"Not since before I left for Mexico."

"How did he appear to you then, Ranger Jones?"

"He looked very sick."

"He has a cancer and he looks even worse now."

"That may be, but I have to find out the reason for all the damage to that young girl."

"Why, Ranger Jones?"

Jones looked at the doctor, puzzled by his question. "Look, Ranger. What I mean is this: I don't expect MacDuff to see spring. In fact, he could die any day now. So you tell me what earthly good would be accomplished by tormenting a sick and dying old man? And what charges could you bring? You have no evidence, just your testimony and this postmortem, which was not even conducted by an American physician."

"He just might confess, and then there would be your testimony on top of it."

"He won't confess, and my testimony would be that I treated the girl for a bad cough and two broken bones."

"But there were more than two broken bones," Jones insisted.

"Yes. According to this report, there were, but I only set two, an arm and a leg, as I recall." Dr. Biesecker got up and went over to a file cabinet. He pulled out a buff-colored folder and brought it back to his desk and removed several sheets of paper. "Yes, here it is. The leg when she was five and a half years of age—she had fallen from a tree—and an arm when she was seven and her pony threw her." He paused, looking intensely at Jones. "I will gladly make all of my records available to a court of law, but I'll be damned if I'll assist you in the harassment of one of my patients!" Doctor Biesecker's face was bright red. He reached for his pipe and began filling it from a pouch of tobacco.

"Doc," Jones said calmly, "it was never my intention to harass him." Jones shook his head. "I thought you would know more about the injuries than you do, so at this point, I have to agree I don't have a hell of a lot to go on. You never saw any signs of beatings or other abuse?"

The doctor held a match to his pipe and puffed until the tobacco glowed red in the bowl. He puffed in silence and looked carefully at Jones. "Ranger, it occurs to me that there are several similarities in our chosen professions. We have to read people and discern the things that they are not telling us. A majority of the time, we use facts and scientific deduction, but there are times when we have to use our instincts. Are you following me?"

Jones nodded.

"You asked me if I saw any signs of abuse, and I must tell you that in the strictest sense of the meaning, I did not. But there was something there that was not right, and if you asked me to describe it, I could not. But based on my observations and conversations over the years with the mother and daughter, I would have to say that the atmosphere was just not normal. Had I known the facts in your good doctor's report, I would have had something more to go on, but as it is, I only treated her for two very common childhood injuries. I never was aware of the others."

Doctor Biesecker leaned back and puffed white clouds of tobacco smoke, deep in thought. "I told you MacDuff would never confess." He put his pipe in the ashtray.

"Yes?" Jones felt he was close to an answer.

"What I meant was that he could never confess, because in my opinion, he did not cause the injuries to the little girl."

"The mother?" Jones's stomach tightened.

"Yes, I think so. There was always tension between them. The young girl was a spirited little thing, but her mother could destroy her with one word or one of her looks, and that often made me wonder about her. I knew that she was not the natural mother of the girl, but I did not, nor do I now, know the background of their relationship. Anyway, that is all I can offer. That and a quarter will get you a haircut and shave across the border."

Jones ran it all through his mind and came to grips with the fact he had been going down the wrong path. The doctor tapped the bowl of his pipe against the side of the ashtray, knocking a small pile of dead ash onto the glass. "And now they are both dead, killed, according to your report, in a most horrible way. And there you have the other similarity in our respective professions ... we both are very familiar with death." The doctor got up from behind his desk and followed Jones to the door. "Did you catch the killers?"

Jones stepped out onto the porch. "We caught 'em, Doc. They won't kill again."

"Good. Very good to hear that. Good night, Ranger." He watched the lawman limp off in the direction of Dominguez Street.

When Jones got back to headquarters, he went in to see Captain Wheeler and report what he had learned from Doctor Biesecker.

"Poor old MacDuff. Makes you wonder if he knew."

"If he did, I'm sure he'll take it with him to the grave, and if Doc Biesecker is right, that won't be long now." Jones handed the captain Dr. Lovato's report.

"I'll file this with your final report. I think Dr. Lovato's finding will speak for itself and there's no need to address the girl's injuries in your report. As far as I'm concerned, this wraps it up. What do you think?"

"I agree. Two of the three parties are dead, and the third soon will be." Jones got up from his chair. He was suddenly very tired. "I have been meaning to ask you about that little place over around Patagonia. Do you remember?"

"Yes, I remember. While you were down in Mexico, it was sold to some easterner who came in and offered them more than it was worth. My friend took the money before the buyer changed his mind. I never told him about you because you didn't show that much interest. Why do you ask?"

"No reason in particular, just curious." Jones's heart sank. "Good night, Captain."

Jones walked out of the office and turned right on Towner Avenue. The sun was down, and the new streetlamps were lit, and even though it was the second week of January, Christmas decorations were still up in several stores. He stopped in front of a general store and stared into the window, not seeing anything, when a cold blast of winter air brought him out of his trance. He noticed the faded red of the Christmas tree bulbs and the dull green of the fake pine boughs in the window display, and he felt his dream of a ranch slowly seep out of him. He had planned on a good meal before turning in, but now he had no appetite. He thought about getting drunk but knew that would be a waste of time, so he walked aimlessly through the streets of Naco in the chill of the evening air and then went back to his room, where he slept, without waking, until dawn.

The rest of January passed slowly, and Jones felt like a prisoner confined to headquarters, but by the beginning of February he felt strong enough to return to the field.

THIRTY-ONE

I t was the second week of February 1909, and for the last month, the Arizona newspapers had been full of stories of the plan by the territorial legislature to dissolve the Ranger force. The front page of the *Arizona Republican* had trumpeted "Rangers on the Run!" Jones read the accounts of the so-called Weedin Bill, which had passed out of legislative council, calling for the abolition of the Arizona Rangers. The articles went on to discuss the individual votes of the legislature and broke down the votes by their political party affiliation. He was tired of hearing about the bill, but like the other lawmen, he began to accept the inevitability of the end of the Ranger Company in spite of the governor's threat to veto the bill.

He had helped Captain Wheeler prepare the monthly report for December, which recorded fifty-eight arrests made by the Rangers that month, fifty-five of them resulting in convictions. It irritated him that none of the facts cited in the report had any effect on the politicians who had decided that the Rangers were not needed. The captain had wired orders for Jones to bring several additional budget reports and join him in Phoenix the next day. He had a ticket on the morning train and had spent the day finishing up several reports and recording two more prosecutions; one for murder and the other for cattle theft. A new recruit had been detailed to assist Sergeant Craig at Ranger headquarters, and Jones could not wait to leave all the administrative duties to them.

He had received a letter from Catalina two days before. She told him she would be in Phoenix at the Hotel Adams on the twentieth and wrote how much she looked forward to seeing him and traveling with him to see the ranch near Patagonia. It was not a long letter, and Jones read it so many times, he practically had it memorized. The thought of meeting Catalina without a job and then having to tell her that the ranch in Patagonia was no longer available set Jones's teeth on edge. An amendment to the Weedin Bill gave sheriffs in the territory the authority to create positions of Special Rangers, but Jones had no desire to work for a sheriff and be limited by county jurisdiction.

He had been unemployed before, but he had never had a reason to hope for a future with someone like Catalina, and since leaving Mexico, he had found himself dreaming like a schoolboy of the future of a life with her. He knew he could never come close to matching what she had financially, but his pride demanded that he should at least be able to eke out a living on his own small place. Even though he knew she would not care about these things, he could not imagine seeing her again with no plans or prospects for the future. Even if they were small compared to her family's holdings, at least they would be his and his alone. He cursed himself for not moving quicker with the bank to buy the ranch, but he could do nothing about it now. All he knew was that she would be in Arizona in six short days and he badly wanted to see her.

The young recruit hated working at headquarters with the two old rangers. He had not joined up to be a damn file clerk, and he was disappointed that old Ranger Jones was nowhere near like the famous lawman in the stories the young man had heard. For one thing, he was older and smaller than he had imagined, and if he was such hot stuff, how had he come to be all beat up and crippled? If a feller got himself into a situation where he got shot and beat to hell, it sure didn't speak for much in the brains department, and since yesterday, Jones had been moping around the office with a real worried look on his face while massaging his right hand like an old granny. Damn, he thought, I can't wait to get out of this office, away from these old farts and into the field, where the action is.

The candlestick telephone on the sergeant's desk rang.

The sergeant let it ring twice before he lifted the earpiece.

"Hello! Who? Oh—OK. It's for you, Owen." He handed the phone to Jones. Jones held the earpiece to his right ear and said nothing. The sergeant handed Jones the candlestick with the mouthpiece. "Speak into this, Owen," the sergeant instructed.

The young man snickered. Jesus! The old fart didn't even know how to use the telephone.

"Hello?" Jones spoke into the mouthpiece. He listened closely as a woman's voice crackled into the earpiece.

"Mr. Jones?"

"Yes?" Jones pulled the mouthpiece closer.

"This is Anabelle Meeks. From Tucson? Do you remember me?"

"Yes, ma'am, I do."

"How are you, Mr. Jones?"

"Well, I'm fine, ma'am. How are you?"

"Fine, Mr. Jones. The reason I'm calling is, well, do you remember our walk and conversation?"

"Yes I do, ma'am."

"And I promised I would call about that gang you were looking for?"

"Yes. I remember."

The recruit walked over to a filing cabinet to hide his smirk and to keep from laughing at the way Jones held the earpiece with his elbow out parallel to the floor, his back stiff as if standing at attention. He doubted the old fart had ever used a telephone before.

"You remember I told you about a feller name of Ezekiel Bent?"

"Yes. I do." Jones felt his insides go cold.

"Well, he's up in Apache County near St. Johns."

"Are you sure?" Jones asked.

"Sure as little green apples. He beat up an employee of a friend of mine, and he is up to something, because my friend tells me that he travels back and forth into New Mexico Territory."

"Will your friend talk to me?"

"Oh, I'm sure she will, Mr. Jones!"

Jones thought he heard a giggle at the other end of the line.

"How can I get in touch with her?"

"Just ask for Natalie at the Rusty Spur in St. Johns."

"When did she last see him?"

"Two days ago. He ain't goin' anywhere. He's got lots of kin in the area, and they're taking real good care of him."

"I'll look into it. Thank you, Miss Meeks."

"You're welcome, Mr. Jones, and be sure and stop by when you're in Tucson."

"I'll do that."

"Goodbye, Mr. Jones."

"Goodbye, Miss Meeks."

Jones placed the earpiece on the desk. Sergeant Craig quietly picked it up and replaced it in its cradle. Jones did not notice. He was not aware of anything in the room. His mind was far away, and it was filled with the face of Ezekiel Bent. The recruit, standing over by the filing cabinet, was still chuckling to himself about Jones's ignorance of the telephone, but when he turned and saw Jones's face, the chuckle died in his throat and he felt a touch of fear. The young man, who prided himself on reading people's faces, could not recognize the look that Jones wore. Was it hatred or anger or a terrible determination? He could not tell, but he was sure of one thing; the gaze in the old man's eyes could cut steel.

Jones got up and left the office without a word. The sergeant turned to the recruit. "Captain Wheeler has arranged for Jones to join him in Phoenix. His train leaves at 9:20 in the morning. I want you to see that his horse and all his tack is on that train. Got that?"

"Yessir, I'll handle it."

Sergeant Craig went back to his paperwork and was pleased to see that the recruit had lost some of his swagger.

Early the next morning, Jones packed his grip and looked around his room to see if he had missed anything. When he was satisfied that everything he owned was in the small grip, he picked it up and went down to settle his bill with the owner of the boarding house. He then walked the few blocks to Ranger headquarters to pick up the captain's papers. Sergeant Craig was waiting for him, and it occurred to Jones that during his entire enlistment with the Rangers, he could not remember a time, day or night, when Craig wasn't on duty at headquarters.

"Our young recruit has seen to your horse and tack."

"Thanks." Jones put the papers in his grip.

"Well, goodbye, Craig. It was good working with you." He and the sergeant shook hands.

"Take care of yourself, Owen, and if the governor can veto this damn thing, maybe we'll see you back here."

Jones walked out of the office and down to the train station. He looked at the store fronts on Main Street and recognized a few familiar faces who nodded in his direction. He hefted the light grip in his left hand and thought that he would probably never return to Naco and smiled at the irony of leaving with all his worldly possessions packed in one small grip.

THIRTY-TWO

━━━◆━━━

S pence stood at the railing, watching the island of San Juan de Ulua pass on his right and looking back at the city of Vera Cruz as it grew smaller in the distance. He had done well in Mexico, but he knew the country was not big enough to hide in, and besides, the rumblings of a coming revolution grew louder every day. Not only that, but he simply could not lay low for any length of time. His need for activity and the thrill of pulling off a scheme was great. The potential of Europe was attractive to him, but it would have to offer quite an adventure to beat the excitement he had enjoyed in Mexico.

He lit a cigar, cupping his hands against the offshore breeze, and thought about the Banco del Mar in Sonora.

Three days before the payroll was due to be shipped, he had arranged a routine visit to his safety deposit box in the basement of the bank. As he had entered the room, he had noted thick velvet drapes on the far wall that covered the double door to the room where the mine payroll was stored. He had set his large valise on the floor by his safety deposit box and crossed the room to the curtains and pulled them aside. He had studied the two locks on the door. One was a dead bolt and the other an integral lock for the door latch. He remembered thinking that the dead bolt, of the latest German design and with opposing tumblers, would be his biggest challenge. In fact, he had defeated it in less than a minute. The integral lock had taken less than ten seconds. He had relocked the doors and, remembering the feel and movements of the cylinder of the dead bolt, had inserted the pick and worked the lock again. The second time, he had gotten it down to twenty seconds. Satisfied with his progress, he had done it twice more just to be sure. He had then stepped into the room and seen the payroll boxes and a large safe.

The American safe and its combination lock had been one that Spence recognized, and he had known that this system was limited to a three-number combination. This particular safe had a reputation among second-story men as a pushover. Spence had gone over to the safe, noted that the combination dial was set at zero, and gently pulled on it to determine if there was any inward or outward play. Any loose play in the dial ring could cause an inconsistency in the turning of the dial and prevent him from feeling feedback from the dial shaft to the dial. The vulnerability of this particular model lay in the imperfection in the casting of the three internal security wheels. All three had to be lined up so that the nose of a lever engaged the cam, which would slide open the door bolts when the safe handle was pulled. Any good safe man could feel the resistance, caused by rough casting, as each wheel gate, which was matched to a number on the dial, rotated to the top, where a bar would slide into the gate. When all three gates lined up, the cam would engage and the bolt would slide back, freeing the door to swing outward on its hinges.

Jimmy Nelsen, who had been acting as Sir James, was one of the best safe men on the planet and would have no problem with this one. Still, Spence had been unable to resist the temptation and had begun turning the dial, carefully feeling the resistance.

He had first turned it counterclockwise and, on the fourth revolution, felt it drag as it neared the number seventeen. He had reversed direction after making a mental note of the number, and on the second revolution, felt a bit more drag at the number twelve. He could feel nothing on the third revolution and after a while gave it up and returned to knob to zero. He knew that Jimmy could easily find the third and last number in the combination.

He had gotten up and opened the strongboxes, found them empty, and then turned and left the room. He had quietly shut the door, reset the locks, and pulled the curtains back into place before moving over to his safety deposit box. He had spent the better part of five minutes emptying the box of papers, currency, and gold. These he placed in his valise, snapped it shut, and re-locked the box.

The next morning, he and Jimmy had returned to the bank and, as he had done the day before, Spence had chosen the early hours of the business day to ensure that there would be little traffic in the basement of the bank. Silva had accompanied them to the entrance to the vault area. He had instructed the guard to unlock the outer door that led into the basement and had watched as Spence unlocked the door into the safety deposit room. After the door was open, Silva had nodded to the guard, who closed the outer door and locked it. Spence had moved quickly to the drapes, and Jimmy had watched admiringly as he had opened the double doors in less than thirty seconds. Spence had pointed to the safe and told Jimmy the first two numbers of the combination. Jimmy had wasted no time in dialing the numbers and then slowly dialed counterclockwise for the third number and smiled as he stopped at the number forty-seven. The lock bar had slid back with a solid clunk, and he swung the large door open. They had both looked in at the stacks of American dollars for a moment before beginning their systematic switch of the real currency with Daniel's counterfeit notes.

The real money was put up in small cloth sacks, each holding ten thousand dollars in twenty-dollar bills. Spence's heart had beat faster as he had opened several sacks to check for money bands and was relieved to see that the bills were stuffed into the sacks with no banding. This would definitely save him time in the exchange. After filling the empty valise with the payroll cash and neatly restacking the sacks, which were now full of counterfeit notes, they had closed the safe door, spun the dial to zero, and walked over to the double doors and through them into the safety deposit room. Jimmy had wiped sweat from his face as Spence relocked the double doors and pulled the curtains back into place. Spence had been calm as they exited the room and gone over to the outer door and knocked for the guard.

They had gone back to the Cuahtemoc and counted out the money in bundles and placed them into American-style bands marked "$2,000." They had each kept one thousand dollars and placed another twenty thousand among the clothes in a large suitcase.

"Did you deposit the pesos from del Castillo?" Spence had asked.

"Yes. I did it yesterday and requested a transfer to the bank's main branch in Mexico City. The transfer will take place today." Jimmy had given a nervous laugh.

"What is it?" Spence had looked at him.

"I was remembering the look of satisfaction on the lawyer's face when he handed me the pesos in exchange for the pound notes."

"Well, he won't have that look when his banker discovers that the pound notes are counterfeit. We need to be out of here before that happens and before the real Sir James returns from Panama."

Spence had laughed. "I'll go to the bank with the dollars and arrange for my own transfer of funds. Do you have my ticket?"

Jimmy had shown Spence the train tickets. "Thanks, Jimmy. I'll meet you at the train depot."

Spence had picked up the valise and made his way to Silva's office at the bank. For all the money it held, he did not think that the valise was that heavy.

He had arranged for the deposit of the cash and the transfer of it and other funds into several banks in Mexico City. It was routine for him to transfer large amounts back and forth to the capital, and Silva always ensured it was done quickly and discreetly.

Spence and Jimmy were in Mexico City one day before the counterfeit payroll began its journey north to Cananea. They had spent the morning arranging the transfer of funds from Mexican branches of English and Spanish banks to their home offices in London and Madrid and then said goodbye at the train station in Mexico City. Sir James, now with two good eyes, no limp, and speaking with a broad Midwest accent, had boarded a train for San Antonio en route to Chicago. Spence had caught the train to Vera Cruz and boarded the ship late that evening.

As he stood at the ship's railing, reliving the adventure, Spence again felt the adrenaline rush through his body. He pulled his watch from his vest pocket and estimated that right about now, the counterfeit payroll was being loaded on the special northbound train.

San Juan de Ulua was sinking into the western end of the Gulf of Mexico as the liner steamed northeast.

Spence felt a hand on his elbow and turned to meet the smile of Ariane Marie D'Argeneau. Her red hair was brilliant in the morning sun, and her blue eyes met his in a blend of mischief and promise. She was absolutely thrilled to be leaving Mexico, which she considered a provincial outpost of civilized Europe and could not wait to return to Paris and resume the lifestyle of the indulged child of a prosperous family of the old aristocracy. She had met this man who she knew as Racicot at a reception at the French Embassy several months ago. He had told her that business would soon take him to London and Paris, and she had simply changed her travel plans to go with him. He was an exciting and mysterious man who, according to her friends at the embassy, enjoyed success as an international businessman. He was urbane and a gentleman who spoke passable French, but somewhere in him, there was a hard edge with a bit of unpredictability.

"Come, darling. I have arranged for champagne and pâté in our cabin. It is so boring watching the water go by." She held onto his arm.

Spence tossed his cigar over the railing into the churning wake of the big ship. He looked at her again and thought she was one of the most beautiful creatures on earth. It would be a pleasant and probably exhausting trip to Southampton. She pulled at his arm, and he followed, captivated by her smile. Her wavy red hair spilled down over her long, elegant neck which was set off perfectly by a bright pearl necklace.

THIRTY-THREE

T he captain had arranged for Jones to stay at Ford Hotel in Phoenix. It was more upscale than most hotels Jones stayed in, and after Jones checked in, he walked over to the territorial capitol to find Captain Wheeler. He found the captain in the legislature gallery and handed him the reports just as the council was leaving for the day.

Captain Wheeler was agitated over something, but he calmly briefed Jones on the status of the Weedin Bill. "There's been a lot of support from the citizens, and the governor said he would send his veto in tomorrow. Several of the legislators who are on our side have asked me to stand by to testify. I think that we have enough support, and I'm confident the veto won't be overridden, but we'll have to wait and see."

"Anything I can do?" Jones was encouraged by the captain's optimism.

"I'd like you to stand by with me and be prepared to talk to the council about the success of your recent experience with the colonel and his outfit."

"I'll do it, but you know that I'm not a good talker."

"Don't worry. If they ask any questions, just answer like you always do." The captain looked over Jones's shoulder and waved to someone. "Look, Jones, I've got to see a few people about these papers you brought. Why don't you take the rest of the day off and relax. I'll see you back here at nine o'clock tomorrow morning."

Jones walked back in the direction of the hotel. He spotted a barber shop and went in for a haircut. He then walked down Washington Street to Boehmers Drug Store.

"What can I do for you, sir?" the man at the counter asked.

"Two cakes of that shaving soap and a spare blade for a Star Safety razor."

"I'm sorry, sir; I sold our last wedge blade the other day. If you'll bring the old blade in, I can have it honed for you."

"It's chipped and can't be honed. What is that?" Jones pointed to a display.

"Well, sir, it's the new Auto-Strop razor. Works like your Star, except it has a thinner blade and you strop the blade while it stays in the razor. It's real convenient and a time saver. It comes with an extra pack of blades and its own strop. One pack of blades will last a year."

"Sounds good, but five dollars is a little too stiff for me."

"Well, sir, it is a new item and I'll be able to knock a dollar off, but you won't get the extra pack of blades."

"OK. I'll take it, but you'll have to show me how to work that strop."

Jones spent a few minutes learning the new stropping method, and then he bought a bag of hard candy and some plug tobacco. He walked around town for an hour, looking in several shops, and then returned to the hotel for supper.

The next morning, he met Captain Wheeler at the capitol and sat with him in the gallery. The council announced it would not meet that morning and would go into session at one o'clock in the afternoon, so the captain took Jones with him to meet with several legislators who promised they would call upon him to testify. With the exception of a few who were ranchers, most of them, in Jones's opinion, had never slept rough or had to catch or kill their supper.

Shortly after one o'clock, Jones's contempt for the legislators grew as they discussed the bill to abolish the Rangers. The representative from Navajo County said that the Rangers were a lot of gun players from Texas and that the citizens of his county were satisfied with their own peace officers. And the author of the bill for abolishment, Mr. Weedin, said that the Rangers were only responsible to the governor, who, in turn, was not responsible to the people of Arizona but to some man in Washington. He then declared that the governor imposed a ten-percent assessment on each ranger's monthly salary that went to his campaign funds.

There were more statements by other politicians. Jones had never before seen people who liked to hear themselves talk so much, and after a short while, he tuned them out in utter disgust. He began thinking about Ezekiel Bent and wondered how the killer had managed to make his way back to Arizona from the high Sierras of Mexico. Would he stay in the St. Johns area? He knew Bent to be a follower, not a leader, who would most likely stay where he was comfortable and not strike out on his own. He was confident that Bent would stay near his kinfolk until either the law caught up with him or one of his kin killed him.

Jones turned his attention back to the talk on the floor of the legislature, but it was over quickly. It was, as one of the newspapers later described it, as if the guillotine had dropped. The legislators voted to override the governor's veto, and the abolition of the Arizona Rangers was to take effect immediately. They never called on the captain to testify, and to add insult to injury, there was to be no period for transition. The lawful authority of the Rangers was to cease that very afternoon, and their pay was to be stopped at the end of the day. The Arizona Rangers simply ceased to exist. It happened so quickly that Jones and the captain sat quietly for a few minutes, stunned by the finality of it all. Then Captain Wheeler slowly pulled himself out of his seat and turned to Jones.

"I reckon I better telegraph Sergeant Craig to get the word out to the men. Damn it, we have rangers chasing rustlers in the Chiricuahuas and it'll be hard to reach them out there. God forbid any of them should come to harm." The captain seemed distracted. "There's nothing we can do now, Owen. I'd best head back to Naco immediately. I'll be making plans for the future, and I do have several opportunities you might be interested in, so stay in touch."

Jones reached in his shirt pocket, pulled out his ranger badge, and handed it to the captain, who looked at it and smiled.

"I hope you have plans to stay in Phoenix tonight, because your room and supper have already been paid by the Ranger budget, so enjoy a last meal and a night's lodging on the Rangers!" He shook Jones's hand.

"Goodbye and good luck, Captain." Jones watched Captain Wheeler walk out of the chamber. The captain held his head high and refused to speak to or even look at any of the legislators.

As Jones walked out of the capitol building, he felt the loss of something more than a paycheck. It was like they had chopped a piece of him off back there in the legislative chambers, and he struggled to right his thoughts. You're still who you are, he thought, you're just not a ranger anymore. It wasn't as if he couldn't pin on another badge. Hell, most sheriffs in the territory would be glad to have him. No. That wasn't it. He looked around himself at the well-dressed townspeople going in and out of the buildings on the capitol grounds and knew that he had to get the hell away from here. He thought about it some more and decided to go and talk with his banker to see if he knew of any good land up for sale.

The banker, after expressing his disappointment in the abolishment of the Rangers, assured Jones that the bank was still willing to carry the note on a piece of land and gave Jones a list of several properties for sale in the valley. All were within a short ride of Phoenix, so Jones made plans to stay in town a couple more days and take a look at some of the property on the list. Catalina wouldn't be in town for five more days, and he made up his mind that he would spend that time trying to find a place where he could begin a new life as a small rancher. He thought about being with Catalina again, but there was a feeling of desperation telling him he had to have something to offer in any plans for the future. He was almost fifty years old and a man with no prospects. He couldn't remember ever feeling this low.

He walked back to his hotel and made arrangements to keep the room for several more days. He had withdrawn two hundred dollars from his bank in case he needed some earnest cash for property, and he felt confident that he had enough in his account to back the purchase of a fair-sized piece of land. At supper in the hotel dining room, he went over the banker's list of properties and eliminated the listings that were either too big or too small. He looked up as Hank, an old friend, came over to his table. Hank was an old Rough Rider, and when he had returned from Cuba, badly wounded, Captain Wheeler had used his influence to get Hank a job as a night watchman in Phoenix. Hank had never been shy about giving everyone within earshot the benefits of his strongly held opinions, so within a few minutes, everyone in the dining room learned what a bone-headed move the legislature had made in abolishing the Ranger Company.

Hank and Jones talked for a few more minutes about current events, and after a bit, Hank excused himself, saying he had to make his rounds. Jones wished him well and went back to studying the property listings.

In the morning, after breakfast, he had the kitchen prepare a sack lunch and then walked down to the livery to get his horse and begin the slow process of riding out to look at the different properties.

After three days of the same routine, he had eliminated all the prospects on the list. Several of the smaller ranches were on well-fenced good grazing land with good water and were reasonably priced. They were also close to the rail line, which would eliminate the need for a long drive to get his cattle to market, but after looking at several ranches on the first day, something began to gnaw on Jones. On the second day, he realized what it was. Despite all the benefits of good grazing and plenty of water, it occurred to him that everything in the valley was too close. He could not leave one ranch without immediately seeing the buildings and stables of the next ranch. Hell, he thought, it's almost like living in town. He thought of the ranch in Patagonia and how he could look out from the building site in all directions and see nothing but good grazing and palo verde between him and the mountains to the south. The only sounds were the wind and the occasional shriek of a hawk as it hunted over the black gramma grass below.

On the third day, he tore up the list of properties as he walked back to the hotel from the livery stables. Thoroughly discouraged, he sat in the hotel dining room, picking at his steak and potatoes. Hank walked through the double doors of the dining room and approached Jones's table with a newspaper in his hand.

"Any luck?" Hank asked.

"Nope." Jones pushed his plate away. "Sit down, Hank."

"Seen this?" Hank handed Jones the newspaper.

Jones looked at the story on the front page and read aloud, "Geronimo laid to rest." The caption was set out in large print.

"Didn't know you were partial to old Geronimo, Hank."

"I wouldn't give two hoots in hell about Geronimo, but it got me to thinking. The Rangers are gone, Geronimo is dead, and pretty soon this damn place will be a state." Hank tapped the newspaper with his finger.

Jones said nothing as he watched the old veteran's face turn red. "I got a nephew, Owen. He's sixteen years old, and you know what he's doing? He's countin' votes over at the legislature. They're paying him good money to carry papers around and count votes for those lazy politicians. Now, what kind of job is that for a young fella? I'd rather he be swampin' out a whorehouse. At least he'd be in better company." Hank shook his head. "Times are changin', Owen, and I'm not sure they're changin' for the best. Seen how many of them automobiles we got in this town? It won't be long before we got more of them than horses. Dammit, I'm starting to sound like an old coot!" He sighed.

The waiter came over to the table and removed Jones's plate. Hank ordered a slice of apple pie and coffee, and he and Jones talked about the Rangers and Hank's time in Cuba and about the possible changes that statehood would bring to Arizona. After a while, they sat quietly sipping their coffee as the supper crowd drifted out of the dining room.

"You gonna be in town long, Owen?"

"Don't know, Hank."

"Well, if you get bored, you can always come with me and shake doorknobs." Hank chuckled and got to his feet. "Gotta start my rounds, Owen. Take care." He held out his hand, which Jones shook.

Jones watched Hank limp out of the dining room and then turned back to the newspaper. Geronimo was to be buried at the Apache burial ground northeast of Fort Sill, Oklahoma. Jones put down the paper and wondered about the fact that both Comanches and Apaches, once mortal enemies who had roamed freely all over the southwest and Mexico, had ended up being forced to live in Oklahoma. Not many men he knew had ever ridden north of the Red River, but they had always considered Oklahoma a place to be avoided at all costs. He began thinking about his own wandering and the fact that he had never been concerned about what the future would bring. The future had always just brought more miles of wandering and with each mile a new adventure. He sipped his coffee and listened to the echoes of Father O'Casey's last words to him about finding his purpose in life, and he began to wonder if he had missed something in his wandering. After giving it some thought, he dismissed this notion, because each mile that had brought a new adventure had also brought him a new purpose. Whether it was tracking down stolen cattle or fleeing desperados, or working as a ranch hand, he had always felt that he was serving a useful purpose.

The dining room was still and quiet with the departure of the evening crowd, and in the calm he could hear, clear as could be, Sergeant Sutton's voice: "By God! I never felt so ready to start the day as I did when we was set against the Comansh."

Jones sat there for a while longer and listened to more voices from his past and wondered if there would come a time for his own Oklahoma but finally gave it all up as a waste of time, dismissed all the ghosts at his table, and began to think about the here and now. He settled his bill and walked out of the hotel and down the street to a newsstand, where he bought a cigar. He lit it and began a slow walk around town. After an hour of walking, he went back to the Ford and walked up to his room.

Jones sat in a chair, deep in thought, then got up and went over to the desk and opened the center drawer. He pulled out several pieces of hotel stationery, squared them on the desktop, and began writing. The first letter, he wrote quickly. It was addressed to Captain Wheeler and gave him authorization to send any money due Jones to his banker in Phoenix. When he was finished, he folded the letter and placed it in a hotel envelope, addressed and sealed it, and then set it aside.

The second letter took much longer. He thought out each sentence very carefully before putting it on paper, and when he was finished, he addressed the envelope to Mrs. Catalina Gallegos de San Martin, care of the Hotel Adams, Phoenix. He sealed the envelope and placed it on the desk next to the other. He then took off his boots and lay down on the bed and was asleep in an instant.

Jones was wide awake at three in the morning. He got up and splashed water on his face, put on his boots and gun belt, and got his rifle and hat from the bed. He picked up his grip, went to the desk, and retrieved the two envelopes. After looking around the room one last time, he walked down to the lobby. He rang the bell for the night man, purchased a postage stamp, and left the captain's letter with the man for mailing. He walked out of the hotel and down the street to the Adams, where he left the letter to Catalina with the impeccably dressed desk man. As Jones walked over the polished marble floor of the lobby, he had a clear picture in his mind of Catalina being completely at ease in this elegant hotel.

He walked through the cold night over to the livery stable and had to go around back to wake the attendant. He settled his bill and added another thirty cents for a sack of oats.

After saddling his horse and tying his grip and the sack of oats behind the cantle of the saddle, Jones mounted and rode through the dark streets to the east end of town. At the edge of the desert, he stopped and pulled on an old, heavy woolen poncho he took from one of the saddlebags.

He was well clear of the valley and riding east along a bare ridge that ran straight as a railroad track when the starlight faded and the eastern sky lightened in the predawn. The outline of the Superstitions stood out off to his right. He turned to face the east, and more of the desert became visible as the sky continued to brighten. The stars disappeared, and the dark of the night sky slowly gave way to the light blue of dawn. He stopped his horse and sat still as the first rays of sun broke over the dark rim of the Mogollon. The rays grew in orange lines against the light blue of the morning sky, and then, as the sun continued its climb, they turned yellow and the lines all came together in one bright sheet that finally pushed the night sky back for good. The colors of life, he thought. These were the colors that he had always depended on to come every day to chase away the dreams and dark thoughts that grew in the night. And then the leading edge of the sun finally broke over the rim of the earth, and its brilliance forced him to look away, but he felt its warmth and his body responded. His joints loosened as they were freed from the cold and his blood flowed freely through his body.

He pulled his hat lower over his eyes and spurred his horse on, riding east to the Mogollon Rim and the wilds of Apache country. There would be coffee and flour at the trading post on the San Carlos River, and he would ask there for an old scout named Chapo to see if he would go with him to hunt the bad man. There was no hurry, and no other duties awaited him. His sense of freedom had returned the moment he had walked out of the hotel, and as each mile passed and the sun climbed higher, there was something else that cleared his mind and filled him with a sharp purpose. It was the promise he had made to himself and a woman and her daughter in a peaceful little glade under a cottonwood tree on the banks of the Rio Sonora.